Dreamwold Castle

Dreamwold Castle

*

Florence Hightower

Houghton Mifflin Company Boston 1978

Library of Congress Cataloging in Publication Data

Hightower, Florence.
    Dreamwold Castle.

    SUMMARY: In need of a friend, Phoebe is flattered
by the overtures of a wealthy schoolmate and becomes
part of her world of lies and even criminal behavior.
    I. Title.
PZ7.H544Dr   [Fic]   78-14562
ISBN 0-395-27158-4

Printed in the United States of America
M   10 9 8 7 6 5 4 3 2 1

Also by Florence Hightower

DARK HORSE OF WOODFIELD

FAYERWEATHER FORECAST

THE GHOST OF FOLLONSBEE'S FOLLY

MRS. WAPPINGER'S SECRET

THE SECRET OF THE CRAZY QUILT

To Tom

Dreamvold Castle

[1]

CARRYING HER SCHOOL BOOKS, her library book, and the
bag of groceries, Phoebe Smith sneaked up the icy driveway to the comparative shelter of the garage at the end
of the ell. Hugging the wall, as burglars do in books,
she made another dash over the snowdrifts along the side
of the ell, jumped down at the back door, opened and shut
both the storm door and the regular door without making a sound, and tiptoed up the backstairs to the third
floor where she and her mother had their apartment.

The whole house belonged to Miss Tarlton and was
one of the finest in all of Denby, New Hampshire. Miss
Tarlton's family had lived in the house ever since it was
built in 1792, and Miss Tarlton knew the history of
everything in it and about it — and a whole lot more —
and told it all at the drop of a hat. The granite for the
foundations had been hewn from the side of Mount Mottrell, which was just to the north of the town and had
once belonged exclusively to the Tarltons. The fanlight
over the front door and the cupola at the peak of the roof
had been designed by Thomas Jefferson himself especially for His Excellency Mr. Mottrell Tarlton, the
builder of the house. Everything about the Tarltons, ac-
cording to Miss Tarlton, was distinguished and superior.
They even had a ghost.

Toward the ghost, because she was not one of the distinguished Tarltons but a poor black woman named Bess,

Phoebe felt friendly. Bess had been the slave of Judge Ingoldsby Tarlton, who flourished (Tarltons didn't just live, they flourished) in the early years of the nineteenth century. She was such a devoted, responsible nurse to the three Tarlton children that their parents could go away whenever they liked and not worry a bit about leaving their children at home. The Judge and Mrs. Tarlton were away, and Bess was in charge in the summer of 1813 when the children all took sick with what turned out to be typhus. Bess sent for the doctor at once, but he lived two towns away and was so busy visiting other typhus cases — they were turning up all over central and southern New Hampshire — that it took him a week to get to Denby. Meanwhile, Bess nursed the children. Because they burned with fever and thirst, she toted bucket after bucket of cold water from the well in the yard, up to the third floor where the children had their quarters. She let them drink their fill and dip their hands and faces in the bucket. Then she sponged their bodies and went back down for fresh water. When the doctor finally arrived, he told her that water was the worst thing she could give a patient with typhus, the accepted medical theory of the time. Later the two little girls died. Bess felt it was her fault, and she hanged herself in the woodshed, which was now the garage. Miss Tarlton knew exactly which beam she had used.

Ten years later, the boy, who had survived the typhus, heard footsteps and splashing sounds on the third floor, as if someone were lugging around a bucket of water that occasionally sloshed over. No one lived on the third floor at that time, and young Ephraim Tarlton

2

went up to investigate. He found nothing — no footprints on the dusty floor, no puddles of water anywhere. He heard the sounds repeatedly for several days. They reminded him of good, kind Bess — for he had heard those same sounds when, as a child, he had waited miserable and feverish for Bess and her buckets of cold well water, and although he was a sensible young man who had no truck with ghosts, he could not shake off a feeling that the sounds had something to do with Bess.

The death of his father, the Judge, in an accident at the tin mine he had been working on Mount Mottrell put all thought of Bess out of young Ephraim's head. He had to make all the funeral arrangements and see to the blocking up of the mine, which was a hazard to sheep and cows and was losing money besides; and, as he went on to settle his father's estate, he discovered that the old man had squandered most of his fortune on foolish schemes — the tin mine was only one of them.

Young Ephraim devoted himself for the next forty years to restoring the Tarlton fortune and raising a large family of his own. From May first to May fourth in 1863, he heard the footsteps and the sloshing again. On May sixth, the news of the Union defeat at Chancellorsville reached Denby, and a day later came the news of the death in action of Ephraim's eldest son. As Ephraim mourned for his son he recalled that he had heard the steps and sloshings that preceded the news of the boy's death once before, long ago, shortly before the death of his father. Ephraim in his old age was more sensible and hardheaded even than in his youth, but he could not gainsay a voice in his heart that told him that faithful

3

Bess had come back before each death to give warning, to try in the only way she knew how to avert the tragedy. Since Ephraim's time, events had shown that the voice in his heart, though it went against all reason and common sense, could not be ignored.

Bess had walked and sloshed for three days in November 1902, before Miss Tarlton's own father had accidentally electrocuted himself in the cupola while he was experimenting with a new telescope. Bess had turned up a few days before Miss Tarlton's elder brother fell at Château-Thierry. She had come again in 1944, a few days before Miss Tarlton's nephew was killed in the Battle of the Bulge.

Phoebe tiptoed up the backstairs, not for fear of rousing Bess, whom she'd have been glad to meet, but for fear of Miss Tarlton, who might pop out any time, her cold blue eyes agleam, to bore Phoebe with the exploits of her wonderful relatives.

Phoebe had had a bellyful of Tarltons, from the first one to come to America right on through to Mr. Charles Tarlton, who had made the third floor into an apartment and then skipped off to do something significant in Japan — if a Tarlton did it, it had to be significant — thus making it possible for Phoebe and Miranda to have the honor of being Miss Tarlton's tenants. Even Miranda, who, in addition to being Phoebe's mother, was a real brain and had antiquarian interests because she was a history teacher, and who said she felt sorry for Miss Tarlton because she was an impoverished gentlewoman — even Miranda got a glazed look in her eye when Miss Tarlton sounded off on her relatives. Phoebe suspected that Mr.

4

Charles Tarlton, who had recently turned up on a surprise visit to his aunt, was as big a bore as she was. He had come up to call on Miranda last night and talked about Japanese painting. Phoebe hadn't listened long. She said she had homework to do and went to bed with a book. Miranda sat up so late listening to him that she had overslept this morning and barely got to school on time. Phoebe wished Miranda didn't think she had to be so polite to these people, just because she lived in their house. After all, she paid rent.

Phoebe reached the top of the stairs without being accosted by Miss Tarlton. She let herself into the apartment, dropped her hat, mittens, and books on the hall table, and dumped the groceries on the kitchen counter. She started to unbutton her coat but thought better of it and went back to the hall to look at the thermometer. As always, the thermostat was set at 80°, and, as always, the thermometer under it registered 62°. Phoebe whacked it with her fist and listened for the whirr of the fan that meant that the furnace had started way below in the basement. There was no whirr. Phoebe whacked the thermostat again for spite. She unzipped her overshoes, rubbed the toe of one against the heel of the other until it worked loose, then with two good kicks she sent the overshoes flying, one after the other, down the hall almost as far as the big front window. She was practicing to hit the window. If it broke, another draft wouldn't make any difference up here, and it would be fun to make Miss Tarlton mad.

How dreary, chill, and utterly miserable the apartment was! Miranda could talk about the modern kitchen and the big, square, beautifully proportioned rooms, and Miranda could have them, along with the Persian rugs, the Japanese screen, the Chinese chests, the Chippendale chairs, and the charming little fireplace. You'd no sooner get warm and cozy in front of it than you had to go down two flights and out into the cold for more wood.

On the September day, four dreary months ago, when Phoebe and Miranda first saw the apartment, it was full of summer warmth and sunshine; and they had snapped it up, worried only that Miss Tarlton would find something wrong with them and not accept them as tenants. In June, Miranda had landed her first teaching job in the high-school division of Denby School for Girls. Denby was an established school, well endowed and distinguished for its academic excellence; and furthermore, Miss Dwight the headmistress, because she wanted Miranda for a teacher so badly, had offered free tuition for Phoebe in the school's junior division.

"Isn't our Miranda a regular dabster?" Charlotte had exclaimed. "She sweeps everyone before her! Even that snooty headmistress has taken a shine to her!". Charlotte was not only Miranda's elder sister, but her devoted protector and fervent admirer. "Our Miranda," she went on, her glasses steaming up with excess of joy, "is riding the crest of the wave!"

While on the crest of the wave, Miranda bought the Goldfinch, a 1952 Studebaker, yellow with black side panels, almost new, and still not all paid for. She asked their friend Ben Barker to teach her to drive. The lessons taxed Ben's patience and Miranda's determination to the limit because, although Miranda almost had an M.A.

6

degree, she had no mechanical aptitude at all. In mid-August, she finally passed her test and got her license. Still shaky on shifting gears, terrified of left turns, and incapable of backing, she set out in the Goldfinch with Phoebe to find a dream house for them in Denby. She knew exactly what she wanted: a small white clapboard house, in a nice neighborhood, near the school, with a lawn, a garden, and a garage for the Goldfinch in back.

The three-hour drive from Putnam Park, the Boston suburb where they lived, to Denby was harrowing for Miranda and an exercise in self-control for Phoebe, who would have loved to drive herself. Ben had taught her a lot while he was teaching Miranda and said she had all the talent Miranda lacked. Unfortunately she was only thirteen. She advised, directed, and encouraged Miranda, and tried to be patient like Ben and not yell at her when she mixed up the gear positions, rode the clutch, raced, stalled, strained, and otherwise abused the Goldfinch. Miranda, for her part, was grateful for Phoebe's help and claimed she couldn't have made the trip without her. Sometimes, on country roads, she even let Phoebe drive, to give herself a rest.

They had found out very quickly that Miranda's dream house didn't exist in Denby. Day in, day out, through the latter half of August, they made the long trek to look at what the various real estate agents offered. They inspected huge, prohibitively expensive mansions, rundown farmhouses (dirt cheap but without plumbing), grubby cottages on the wrong side of the tracks, evil-smelling apartments over or under stores, and back rooms with shared bath and kitchen. From "crest of the wave" Miranda sank to "depths of despair." No wonder Miss Tarlton's apartment seemed like a godsend! There was a garage, and the rent was reasonable.

How hard poor Miranda had tried to make a good impression on Miss Tarlton, who told them — none too politely, Phoebe thought — that she was taking strangers into her home for the first time and wouldn't put up with just anybody. How patiently Miranda had listened while Miss Tarlton boasted about her house and her family. Miss Tarlton, on the other hand, after expatiating on the virtues of the nephew who fell at the Battle of the Bulge, didn't even listen when Miranda tried to tell her that her husband had been in the Battle of the Bulge too and had been wounded and won a Purple Heart. Phil was killed later in Korea. Phoebe knew it hurt Miranda to have Phil's heroism ignored that way, but Miranda just winced, bit her lip, and went on being polite.

As soon as Miss Tarlton made up her mind to take them as tenants, Miranda bounced right up on the crest of the wave again. Back in the Goldfinch, she hugged and kissed Phoebe and then took her to lunch at the Mottrell Arms in Denby, the fanciest restaurant Phoebe had ever been in, with white tablecloths, cocked-hat napkins, gleaming goblets, and a lighted candle on each table even though it was the middle of the day. While they ate lobster salad and drank iced tea, Miranda told Phoebe about her long-range plan. She would work very hard at her teaching and her M.A. thesis, so that at the end of the year Miss Dwight would give her a five-year contract; and then, because by then they would know the right people in town, they could find the sort of house they wanted; and they'd persuade Charlotte to rent or sell the old house in Putnam Park and move her dressmaking business to Denby, where the rich ladies would appreciate her beautiful gowns and bridal creations much more than the poor ones in Putnam Park ever did and pay more for them too; and they'd all live together in beautiful Denby, more happily than ever before.

Miranda was hard to resist when she believed something and wanted to make you believe it, too. She bent toward you, she gestured with both hands, her cheeks flushed, her dark eyes glowed, and the winning words flowed from her lovely red lips. Miranda was darker and much prettier than either Charlotte or Phoebe, who both had plain brown hair and greenish eyes. Miranda had the gift of gab, too. As Charlotte said, she swept everyone before her. She certainly swept Phoebe before her at lunch and later, when she let her drive the Goldfinch part of the way home. Yet, even on that sunny day in September, Phoebe wasn't absolutely certain that moving to Denby and going to Denby School for Girls was going to be as wonderful as Miranda made out.

[2]

ALL HER LIFE up till now, Phoebe had lived with Miranda, Charlotte, who wasn't married, and Rags, Charlotte's cocker spaniel, in the Stebbins House in Putnam Park. Putnam Park had seen better days before the city closed in around it; and the house, Charlotte's and Miranda's only legacy from their parents, was old-fashioned and shabby, squeezed between three-deckers, with no yard in front and only the tiniest little bit in back for the clothesline. It certainly couldn't compare with the fine houses and gardens of Denby, but Phoebe had been happy in it, with Charlotte worshiping the ground she walked on and loving her all to pieces — for that was the way Charlotte always talked — and Miranda more like a beloved older sister than a mother. In Putnam Park they were known as the Stebbins Girls, and Phoebe wasn't a child, an inferior; she was the youngest Stebbins Girl.

For a while, after he came back from the Second World War, Phoebe's father, Phil, had lived with them and gone to medical school on his G.I. Bill of Rights. Phoebe remembered him in flashes, like disconnected scenes from a movie. He and she were picking up Charlotte's fabric scraps from the dining-room floor, and they were doing it the way Rags did, on all fours, with their teeth. Charlotte sat at the sewing machine, her face as pink and plump as her pincushion; her glasses flashed, and she rocked back and forth laughing, until her hair, which she wore in a plain bun at the back of her neck, fell down. Phoebe and Phil tried to pick up the hairpins with their teeth too, only by now they were laughing so hard they couldn't, and Rags was jumping and barking.

Some time later, Phil had brought Phoebe downstairs in her nightgown in the middle of the night. The whole downstairs, even the kitchen, was full of people, eating, drinking, laughing, dancing, singing, celebrating Phil's graduation from medical school. Miranda, like a fairy princess in a rose-colored dress, and Charlotte, in green, looking sort of dazed without her glasses but smiling all over, were passing the things to eat and drink. Everyone gathered around Phoebe, saying how cute she was, offering her sips and tastes, trying to make her talk, but she was still very young. She just giggled and hid her face on Phil's shoulder.

Charlotte, Miranda, and Phoebe were all at the airport, saying goodbye to Phil. He was a doctor now, and a major, and he was going to Korea to take care of the wounded soldiers. Phil was carrying Phoebe across a big field, and she was running her fingers over the gold insignia on his collar, and the long rainbow row of campaign ribbons, and the Purple Heart on his chest.

He never did come back from Korea. He was killed in a plane crash soon after he got to Seoul. There followed dismal times, when Miranda was crying upstairs, and Phoebe and Charlotte were crying in the kitchen, and Rags was howling with them. However, the dismal times were soon over, it seemed to Phoebe, and she was going to school, and Miranda was going to college, and Charlotte was sewing away at wedding gowns and bridesmaids' costumes, which made beautiful scraps for dolls' dresses, and Ben Barker was coming around often and calling Phoebe "Skibootch," for no reason but to make her laugh, and taking her out to ride in his red-white-and-blue taxi, and buying her ice-cream cones. For seven years, life had gone on like that.

Miranda did so well in college that she decided to go for an M.A. Her pension from Phil paid for it. Charlotte's Bridal Creations flourished. Ben's single red-white-and-blue taxi grew into a fleet. Phoebe always did well in school, but her real interests were at home with Charlotte and Miranda. She knew all about Charlotte's brides and their gowns, and about Miranda's courses, tests, papers, and flames, as Charlotte called them. Miranda had no use for any of the flames — or callow kids, as *she* called them. Phoebe became adept at opening the door, announcing to the callow kid outside that Miranda was not at home, or too sick to see visitors (which might or might not be true), accepting the flowers, book, or candy which the callow kid offered, and shutting the door politely, but firmly, in his face.

The only flame that Miranda allowed to hang around was Ben. They would have had a hard time keeping the house in repair without him, and no one was quite sure if he was Miranda's flame, or Charlotte's or possibly Phoebe's. He always took Phoebe to the movies along with the others, even if the movie was the sort that children aren't supposed to like, but Phoebe did. While Ben was making repairs around the house, he talked to her as if she were a grownup, and she understood the long arguments he had with Miranda about, among other things, whether it was better to abandon Putnam Park to urban blight (a new expression Miranda had brought home from college) or to try to rehabilitate it. Dear Charlotte didn't understand the arguments nearly as well as Phoebe did, and Phoebe couldn't help smiling when she'd exclaim: "Now isn't that so?" or "I never would have thought of that in a million years!" or, if Miranda and Ben began shouting at each other, "After all, I guess everybody has a right to his own opinion, doesn't he?"

Grownups talked on and on. Phoebe listened only for as long as they amused her. When they got dull, she just sloped off into a book or a daydream. She had read all sorts of books in her time, starting with *The Happy Hollisters,* continuing through all the *Anne of Green Gables* books and on and on: books about dogs, horses, travel and adventure in foreign lands, popular biographies and best sellers even, which Charlotte got out of the library and read too, though Charlotte always shook her head and clucked her tongue disapprovingly over the sex, and the blood, and the detailed descriptions of childbirths and loathsome diseases, which she didn't think Phoebe should read, but Phoebe did anyway — and found them very interesting.

Out of her reading and the many films she had seen (thanks to Ben), Phoebe made up daydreams of her own, more entrancing even than the originals which inspired them. She altered favorite characters to fit herself into their roles, or she added herself as a new character to a story and modified it to suit. She was forever enlarging, embroidering, and improving old stories to fit her own changing moods and tastes. She fought with General Custer as a U.S. cavalry officer, and against him as an Indian brave. She scourged the cities of Asia and Europe with Genghis Khan, and she miraculously escaped murder at his hand to rise up and wreak vengeance. She loved and was adored, and/or betrayed by Lord Nelson, General Montcalm, Sir Francis Drake, and a host of other famous men. She contracted and usually recovered from all the most repulsive diseases.

For over a year, since, to be exact, May 28, 1953,

13

when Edmund Hillary and Tenzing Norkay had climbed to the top of Mount Everest, she had been a Himalayan climber. She hadn't just read about the final conquest of Everest. She had read about the earlier unsuccessful assaults and about assaults on other great Himalayan peaks as well. Mallory, Irvine, Finch, Norton, Shipton, Lambert, and Hermann Buhl were her climbing companions along with Hillary and Tenzing, and of them all she loved Tenzing best. She had spent happy hours working out the details of their courtship and marriage in the wild highlands of Nepal. The fact that Tenzing was comfortably settled with a wife and two daughters (about her age) in Kathmandu didn't faze her at all. In her daydreams anything was possible.

The old house in Putnam Park had abounded in nooks, corners, and cubbyholes — her caves, as Phoebe called them. When things went wrong at school or at home, when being a full-time Stebbins Girl became a burden, she retired to one of her caves to lose herself in books or dreams. Troubles vanished; hours slipped by like minutes. Suddenly Charlotte was calling her to set the table for supper. The old house was always warm. Charlotte kept it at 80° on account of the customers who came in for fittings. The hot air surged up out of the registers, buoying you up, so you seemed to float on a tropical breeze. The sound of Charlotte's sewing machine was like the soft murmur of insects on a summer day.

[3]

IN MISS TARLTON's fine, cold mansion, each room had exactly four corners. There wasn't so much as a recess for Charlotte's sewing machine (were Charlotte, by some happy miracle, to come to stay with them), let alone a cave for Phoebe. In all the apartment, there was no warmth, no comfort, nothing to make you feel at home. Phoebe glared down the hall to where it was split wide open by the well of the front staircase, which they weren't allowed to use but out of which Miss Tarlton might pop any time she felt like it.

Phoebe's glare softened, and she felt like crying, as she suddenly remembered that one happy day when Charlotte and Ben and Rags had come up out of the stairwell, like three beautiful miracles. It was late on a Sunday morning in October. Phoebe and Miranda were lingering over breakfast and the Sunday paper in the kitchen, when they heard Miss Tarlton.

"Yoo hoo, Mrs. Smith, you have visitors."

They rushed into the hall to see who could possibly be visiting them. Miss Tarlton's Sunday hat was just rising up out of the depths.

"In future, Mrs. Smith, you must make it clear to your friends that they are to use the back door. I was about to leave for church when I heard the bell. Of course, I let them in and showed them up, but I cannot, in general . . ."

Charlotte appeared out of the lower gloom. With cries of joy, Phoebe and Miranda rushed right down past Miss Tarlton to hug and kiss Charlotte, take her parcels from her, drag her the rest of the way up, and hug and kiss her some more. When they came to their senses enough to realize that Ben, with Rags in his arms, was behind Charlotte, they welcomed the two of them only slightly less enthusiastically. Ben struggled to hang on to Rags, who wiggled and yapped and finally popped out of his arms to the floor, and then, for all his weight of flesh and years, shinnied right up Phoebe's stomach to lick her face.

Miss Tarlton interrupted to say that, if the gentleman would come downstairs with her, she would show him where, at the back of the house, he could direct the driver to leave his taxi, and the backstairs by which he could then return to the apartment.

Ben replied that *he* was the taxi driver, and he'd be happy to park the taxi anywhere Miss Tarlton told him to, and he had no objection to using the backstairs. He added in his straightforward way that he'd never been inside such a fine house before, full of such fine furniture, and he guessed that by using the backstairs in a big house like this he'd see a lot more that he'd never have guessed was there. He gazed around, full of curiosity and admiration.

Miss Tarlton turned pale. She gripped the stair rail and caught her breath. "If you have gained entrance to my house under false pretenses in order to rob me, I assure you you won't get away with it!" Her voice trembled, but her eyes blazed.

"Ben isn't a thief," cried Miranda. "He is our friend."

Ben didn't turn a hair. He addressed Miss Tarlton with great respect. "I assure you, madam, I am not offended. I understand your feelings. If I owned as fine a place as this, I would be nervous about thieves too; and, I admit it, taxi drivers have had the reputation of being pretty rough types. However, since the war, many veterans of the highest character have gone into the taxi business. Taxi driving is no longer the disreputable occupation it once was." He went on to explain how he personally checked out a man's character before he hired him as a driver, and about how particular he was as to the cleanliness and mechanical performance of every taxi in his fleet. The taxi outside was a new model. He'd wanted to try it out on a long trip and get passenger reaction to it. That was why he had driven his friends out in it today. He was sorry to have frightened Miss Tarlton and delayed her. He wondered if she would allow him to drive her to church before he parked the taxi in back. He made a bow worthy of Sir Francis Drake himself and offered Miss Tarlton his arm. She accepted the arm with a regal inclination of her hat, and they descended the stairs together.

As soon as the front door had closed behind them, the three Stebbins Girls fell on each other's necks, helpless with laughter.

"Dear Ben," gasped Miranda between bouts of giggling. "He knew how to handle her!" They all laughed and laughed until Phoebe developed hiccups and Charlotte lost every single hairpin. Miranda seemed to have laughed all her awe of Miss Tarlton right out of her. While they were trying on the new jumpers that Charlotte had run up for them, and while Charlotte was being shown the apartment, Miranda kept remembering stories about Miss Tarlton and her relatives and her ancestors and telling them in such a comical way that all three dissolved again in laughter.

After a long time, Ben came back. On the way to church Miss Tarlton had shown him all the sights of Denby, then she had invited him to attend the service with her, which he had done. After the service, she had introduced him to Mr. Bartlett, the minister, and shown him all the Tarltons in the graveyard. On the way home she had directed him to the Mottrell Arms so he could make a reservation to take his friends there for lunch. When he mentioned to her that he'd like to climb Mount Mottrell in the afternoon but was afraid he wouldn't have time, Miss Tarlton told him about the Old Tarlton Trail to the Old Tarlton Tin Mine. It was the quickest and most direct route up Mount Mottrell from the Denby side. After you reached the mine the trail stopped, but you could easily scramble to the top. She explained that, since the state had developed the other side of the mountain with new trails and ski lifts, no one went up the Old Tarlton Trail anymore, and only a few old inhabitants still knew it was there. She even drew a map for Ben, so he couldn't get lost.

"She's a nice old lady," he said, "once she gets over being snooty and suspicious. She likes to talk, and I guess her friends and relatives don't come to see her much, and she doesn't have a car, poor thing, so she can't visit around. I like her, and I feel kind of sorry for her."

He pretended not to understand why the Stebbins Girls, between hoots of laughter, accused him of sweeping Miss Tarlton off her feet, turning her head, and capturing her heart. If he wasn't careful, they went on, he'd find himself being sued for breach of promise before Miss Tarlton's cousin the judge, and he'd end up either hitched to Miss Tarlton or behind bars. Again they couldn't stop laughing. Finally Ben began to laugh too. He told them that if they didn't hurry up and get ready to go out to lunch, he'd take Miss Tarlton instead.

Lunch was delicious: roast beef au jus, with all sorts of hot rolls and pickles and jams and jellies passed around extra and free of charge. Phoebe had an Old Mott (the local nickname for Mount Mottrell) Special Sundae for dessert. This reminded Ben that he had better get started on his climb. He asked Phoebe to go with him.

Ben left Miranda, Charlotte, and Rags off at Denby School for Girls so Miranda could show Charlotte around. He and Phoebe drove through town, then turned off the main road onto narrower and narrower side roads, through thicker and thicker woods, until the taxi could go no farther. Phoebe was sure they were lost, but Ben consulted Miss Tarlton's map and said they were right where they should be. They set off on foot up the two ruts which were all that was left of the road. The day was fair and chilly. Above them, the leaves that were still on the trees burned gold, red, and amber; and they kicked and crunched along through a six-inch carpet of dead leaves.

For all her imaginary explorations, Phoebe had never been in a real forest before. She found the bare black trunks and the prickly evergreens equally sinister, and the slanting, heatless rays of the sun filled her with foreboding. She remembered Hansel and Gretel and the Babes in the Wood and hoped Ben really knew where he was going. The track went on, getting narrower and steeper until it came out of the woods onto a scraggy slope that was steeper than ever; and it zigzagged on up between scrubby bushes and boulders. Ben set a pace that soon had Phoebe panting, but he never rested until they had scrambled onto a sort of terrace built out from the slope of the mountain. Ben consulted his map.

"This must be where the mine was. It's a fine view, and I like being alone up here, where no one ever comes." He looked about him, breathing deep, smiling. "Listen," he said. "You can hear the silence."

Phoebe was too tired to answer him, or to take much interest in the view or the silence.

"Well, Skibootch, shall we go on?" Phoebe looked up, hoping to see the summit just above them, but all she could see was the top of a rocky shoulder.

"It's too far," she said.

"An hour at the most, and another hour back down from the top to the taxi."

Phoebe sighed.

"Come on, Skibootch! You can't desert me now. Pretend it's Everest. That'll make it easier. Khumbu Ice Fall, Khumbu Glacier, Lhotse Face, South Col! Remember the film? You were crazy about it. We saw it three times."

Those glorious names raised Phoebe's spirits, though they didn't restore her wind. Pointing to the shoulder above them, she gasped, "We'll make Camp Six up there." She looked down and noticed a sprawl of odd-looking buildings just at the foot of the mountain, and she couldn't help laughing.

"Thyangboche Lamasery. It looks just like it."

"Everything is where it should be," replied Ben. "Onward!"

"You're Hillary," returned Phoebe. "I'm Tenzing." She was feeling much stronger.

"O.K., Tenzing, old pal," said Ben. "Today we're conquering Everest."

Phoebe followed Ben up a gully and over a ledge to the top of the shoulder, and they saw the summit, a mound of bare rock; between it and them lay a waste of minor peaks and valleys.

"South Col," shouted Phoebe. She adjusted her oxygen mask, glanced down at the flags rolled around her ice axe, and scrambled on after Ben. From below, someone whistled a phrase of music and stopped in the middle. Someone else took up the phrase and finished it. Ben stopped. A moment later the two halves of the phrase were whistled again, in the same way.

"I could have sworn there was no one here but us," said Ben.

Phoebe was inspired. "It's two Abominable Snowmen calling to each other."

Ben laughed. "Right you are, Tenzing, but I wouldn't have thought they could whistle a tune," and he started to climb again.

In what seemed no time at all, Hillary and Tenzing had disposed of all the minor peaks, and Tenzing was unfurling his three flags on the summit. There were no other climbers to be seen. Hillary and Tenzing gazed out in splendid solitude over the top of the world. The sun was setting as they slid, jumped, and scrambled down the open slopes. They jogged through the deepening shadows of the woods to the taxi.

In town, Ben stopped at the drugstore for cigarettes and treated Phoebe to an ice-cream cone for old times' sake. When they came out of the store, a man was walking around Ben's taxi, looking it over. He smiled at them, and Phoebe recognized him as the policeman (out of uniform now) who directed traffic at the crossroads in front of the library every afternoon.

"My name is Wade. I'm the Chief of Police here in Denby." He came up to Ben, holding out his hand. "I've been admiring your taxi. It's a beautiful machine. We could use a few taxis in this town. They'd save the Force a lot of emergency calls that aren't really emergencies." He smiled.

For all it was so late, Ben couldn't resist opening the hood to show Mr. Wade the engine. Then he pointed out the heavy-duty shock absorbers in back, and the extra space for luggage. Mr. Wade liked everything Ben showed him. He asked Ben how he happened to have come way out to Denby. When Ben explained that he had come to visit Phoebe and her mother, Mrs. Smith, and that he and Phoebe had just climbed Mount Mottrell by the Old Tarlton Trail, Mr. Wade became more friendly than ever. He was one of

the few old-timers who still knew about the Old Tarlton Trail and the Tin Mine, and it seemed he
knew Phoebe too. He said he'd noticed her coming
downtown afternoons and going into the library and
the A&P. He said it might seem odd to Ben that the
Chief of Police would spend his time directing traffic,
but Mr. Wade had special reasons for being there at
the crossroads. It was his way of keeping an eye on
things in Denby. He liked to stop trouble before it
started. He said he was especially glad to meet Phoebe.
He'd already had her typed as a nice, quiet kid who read
a lot and helped her mother with the shopping. Now she
turned out to be a climber too! He said he guessed
Ben was lucky to have a friend like Phoebe.

Ben said, "Yes sir, you can say that again!"

Phoebe blushed and licked her cone and tried to look
modest, although she was bursting with self-satisfaction.
Ben realized how late it was. They both shook hands
with Mr. Wade and said good-bye.

Since that day, Ben and Charlotte and Rags had
never come back again.

[4]

PHOEBE STOOD NOW in the cold empty hall by the back
stairwell and reflected that for her, happiness in Denby
had lasted exactly one day. A few tears trickled down
her cheeks. She and Miranda hadn't intended it to be
this way. They had planned to visit Putnam Park al-

most every weekend. That was what the Goldfinch was for. Every weekend, though, Miranda had to take study halls for the boarding students, or chaperone them on trips to museums or concerts or to the dances at some boys' school in Paxton; and she had her courses to prepare and her papers to correct besides. Miss Dwight was a regular slave driver. Except for that once, Charlotte had been too busy to come to Denby.. Almost every Saturday and Sunday there was a wedding for which she made the dresses, and Charlotte always helped her brides and bridesmaids to dress, so she could make last-minute alterations. She always stayed on through the ceremony and reception too: in case of emergency, she said, but also, Phoebe knew, because she had such a good time. She used to slip some of the little cakes and sandwiches into her purse to bring to Phoebe. They were pretty mashed by the time Phoebe got them, but how good they had tasted!

Phoebe wiped away her tears with her sleeve and shook herself. There was no point in spoiling this stolen afternoon with sad memories. She marched into her bedroom and took a key from the back of her bureau drawer. Proceeding into the bathroom she unplugged the new electric heater which Miranda had bought to take off the early morning chill. Miss Tarlton didn't know about the heater. Miranda had said that Miss Tarlton would just fuss over the old wiring and the electric bill, and for the rent they were paying they deserved a lot more heat than they were getting. With the key and the heater, Phoebe went to the front of the hall and unlocked the door to a stairway which was partitioned off and went up at a steep angle into the cupola at the top of the roof. She plugged the heater into an electric socket that Miss Tarlton's father must have had installed before he electrocuted himself with his telescope, and then looked out the windows at the view. From here, she could see over the bare treetops and the steeples and snow-splotched roofs of Denby to the white fields scattered with farmhouses, and beyond them, to Old Mott himself.

He was only 3000 feet high, but massive and craggy. Fires set by early settlers — sometimes by mistake, sometimes to burn out wolves — had burned the timber off Old Mott's summit, whereupon the soil had blown and washed away, leaving him as majestically bald as if he rose high above timber line. His appearance of loftiness was enhanced by his being the only mountain of any size in the vicinity. He towered above the town and the country 'round. Now, stripped of leaves, clad in snow and ice, with blizzards sweeping over him, he was formidable indeed. Phoebe felt no urge to climb his slopes. Accomplished daydreamer that she was, she could transform him into Everest and assault him from the north or the south, as the spirit moved her, without leaving her Eagle's Nest right here in the cupola.

She felt a beam of warmth on her shins. The coil of the heater was nearly all red. She hurried down to the kitchen and unpacked the groceries. The pork chops and a can of applesauce for supper went into the refrigerator, the frozen peas and ice cream into the freezing compartment. She opened the box from the bakery, cut a slice out of the chocolate cake and put it on a plate, then stowed away the rest of the cake and opened a bottle of orange soda. With the cake and the soda, and her library book from the hall table, she climbed back into the Eagle's Nest, set everything down on the floor, and went back down the stairs to close the door and lock it, in case Miss Tarlton were to come prying around.

The cupola did not go with the apartment: Miss Tarlton had been very definite about that. When they moved in, the door was locked, and Phoebe had relieved the tedium of many a long afternoon alone by trying various keys in the lock until she found the right one in a jar on the living-room mantel. The first time she climbed into the cupola, she was almost blinded by the light pouring in from all sides through all eight windows. It wasn't a bit like a cave, but it was warm and confined, and she recognized it right away as a refuge. She also recognized that she must not tell Miranda about it. Overworked as she was, and scared of offending Miss Tarlton, Miranda could not be counted on for sympathy.

Phoebe would rather have shared her discovery with Miranda; they used to share everything, and deceiving Miranda made her decidedly uncomfortable. She glanced at her watch: three o'clock. At five she would clear out, lock up, put the heater back in the bathroom. By the time Miranda got home at five-thirty, she'd have started the potatoes and pork chops. Miranda would be grateful.

The Eagle's Nest was comfortably warm now, though stray breezes were always sneaking in, and the windows rattled constantly. Phoebe took off her coat and settled herself in a dilapidated easy chair which she supposed Miss Tarlton's father had sat in. She was glad his telescope had been removed; it would have taken up all her leg room. By propping her feet on a windowsill, she was able to balance both her book and her plate of cake on her stomach. She set the orange soda within easy reach on the floor and proceeded to leaf through the book. It was called *Alone to Everest*, but it was disappointing. The first half was about climbing in Africa, not about Everest at all. Phoebe had to remind herself that she had been lucky to get the book! Someone else in Denby was a Himalaya freak. Whoever it was was always taking out the books Phoebe wanted. There were lots she hadn't read because the Putnam Park Branch Library didn't have anywhere near so many books as the Denby Library had, and new expeditions were going all the time, and new books were being written about them. She had gotten in the habit of stopping at the library almost every afternoon after school to grab up Himalaya books as soon as they came in. Miss Hawkins, the librarian, had become a friend, as had Mr. Wade, who always asked after Ben and often left his traffic circle in the middle of the street to chat with her. Miss Hawkins and Mr. Wade were the best friends she had in Denby, and today Miss Hawkins had saved this new book especially for her. Today, too, without meaning to, Miss Hawkins had given her an awful scare.

[5]

"You're early," Miss Hawkins had said, eyeing Phoebe with what struck her as unwonted sternness over the circulation desk. "You aren't playing hooky, are you?" Phoebe had frozen in her tracks, certain that somehow someone had sent a message from the ski slopes on the far side of Old Mott to Miss Hawkins, ordering her to apprehend Phoebe Smith, who was cutting her ski class without an excuse. Soon the gym teacher or, worse yet, Miss Dwight, would stride into the library to lead Phoebe away to the punishment she knew she deserved.

"Don't look so scared," Miss Hawkins had smiled. "I was just joking. I've got a surprise for you." She had reached under the counter and brought out the new book. Phoebe had almost fainted from relief. Even now, safe in the Eagle's Nest, she shivered just from remembering. She stuffed her mouth with cake and looked out at Old Mott; however, in her mind's eye she saw not the Himalayan face before her but the other side, the side with the ski slopes, the lifts moving straight up, the serpentining trails, and the skiers darting, weaving, whizzing down.

How she had wanted to weave, dart, and whiz too, and how humiliating it was to be the only girl her age still in the snowplow class! Phoebe couldn't even grab hold of the rope tow without going so stiff with fear that she fell off and lay on her back like a beetle, waving her useless skis in the air, unable even to roll out of the way before the next skier on the rope ran her down. The whole tow had to be stopped while she untangled herself and got out of the way. After she had floundered through the deep snow back to the bottom, carrying her skis on her shoulder the way the gym teacher had taught her, so that they rubbed the side of her neck raw, she was expected to put them back on and start all over. When the teacher had finally hauled her to the top of the tow, her legs were trembling so that she couldn't control them, and she fell on purpose and didn't try to get up, but coasted down on her seat — "like a baby," the gym teacher said. The worst of it all was that Miranda had bought her skis and poles and boots, all very expensive, for Christmas because Phoebe was so sure she wanted to ski. She couldn't tell Miranda that skiing hadn't turned out right, that it was one more thing she was no good at, along with tennis and field hockey and arithmetic and French. Miranda was always so sure that if Phoebe just tried, she'd be good at everything. Miranda just didn't know. She didn't know either that at school Phoebe's nickname was Feeble.

Grimly, Phoebe admitted to herself that it was apt. She was too feeble to go through another afternoon of terror, cold, and humiliation. She had sneaked off while they were waiting for the buses to come to take them to the slopes. No one had missed her, but there would be trouble tomorrow for sure.

She took a long swig of orange soda and tried to forget skiing and concentrate on the book, but she couldn't find where Africa ended and the Himalayas began, and skiing wasn't her only trouble. There was a test on square roots tomorrow, and only this morning Miss Parsons, her favorite teacher, had taken her aside to say that, although she enjoyed the compositions Phoebe wrote about imaginary adventures in foreign lands, she wanted Phoebe's next composition to be about something she had really seen and felt herself. Until Phoebe learned to observe accurately and describe her observations, she would have no real experience on which to base her writings. Her compositions, though they showed a good command of English and wide reading, didn't quite ring true. They verged, and Miss Parsons had smiled very kindly, on plagiarism, which was copying what someone else had written and pretending you'd written it yourself.

Now, for the first time, it was obvious to Phoebe that Miss Parsons had never liked her compositions. She had just pretended to because (unlike that gym teacher) she was kind. She hadn't meant to pin that awful nickname onto Phoebe either, but she had. She had been giving an example of alliteration and, trying to encourage poor, feeble, copy-cat Phoebe (Phoebe understood it all now), had said, "Far from feeble are the fanciful fictions Phoebe fabricates." Everyone laughed and asked her to say it again, and this time her tongue slipped and, without meaning to, she said what she really thought: "Fairly fibby are the fanciful fictions Feeble fabricates." The other girls had just about laughed themselves sick over that, and they'd called her Feeble ever since.

Those girls, with whom Miranda had so hoped she would make friends, and who were more remote and unassailable than Mount Everest itself, began to parade through Phoebe's head, with their horses, dogs, tennis rackets, hockey sticks, skis, and boyfriends, their skill with French and fractions, their jokes, their private laughter, their good manners, and their kindness. The good manners and kindness were hardest to bear. They would never scream dirty words at you, or pinch you, or pull your hair, or spit at you, the way the tough kids sometimes did in Putnam Park. They were well brought up, and anyway they didn't care. At first they had asked Phoebe polite questions and shown her around. Some came over to look at the apartment, and some even invited her to come home with them after school, but it didn't take them long to realize how feeble Phoebe was; and then they left her alone, which was the politest and kindest thing they could do. Phoebe sighed. In a way, if it weren't for Miranda and her high hopes, she wouldn't mind being left alone. She suspected that getting to be friends with those girls wouldn't be worth the trouble. They'd never be to her what Miranda and Charlotte and Ben and Rags had been in the old days.

Phoebe closed her book and stared gloomily at Old Mott. Nothing was working for her today. She was wasting her precious stolen afternoon suffering all her miseries over again. She put the book aside, gathered up the empty bottle and plate, and descended to the kitchen to see if more food would do her any good.

[6]

PHOEBE WAS JUST cutting herself a slice of cake when she heard a knock on the back door.

"Miss Tarlton," she thought, "and I've left the door to the cupola open!" She scurried off to shut it and lock it and hide the key under the bottom step before she went to the back door and opened it. There stood a tall, well-dressed man holding a package.

"Is Mrs. Smith at home?" he asked.

"No," replied Phoebe, "but I'll give her the package," and with the ease of practice she reached to take the parcel and prepared to shut the door. But this was no callow kid. He did not hand over his parcel, and he marched right past her into the hall. She glared at him.

He was not at all fazed. Indeed, he seemed amused. "My, you do take care of your mother," he murmured with a quizzical smile. "I guess you didn't look at me very carefully last night when I was here. I am Charles Tarlton."

Phoebe recognized him now and noticed that the eyes behind his egghead, horn-rimmed glasses were the same icy blue as Miss Tarlton's. She had no intention of encouraging him. She did not smile. She kept silent.

He eyed her doubtfully. "I hope I didn't frighten you. If I just barged in, I guess it's because I forgot that I don't live here anymore. I did use the backstairs, and I did knock. I didn't rise up out of the front stairwell like poor Bess's ghost. You should give me credit for that." He tried another smile. Phoebe remained stern. "Come to think of it though," he added, "poor Bess would use the backstairs, and I expect she knocks, or taps before she comes in. You didn't mistake me for Bess, did you?" His smile and his tone were friendly enough but Phoebe wasn't about to be cajoled by a Tarlton.

"No, I didn't," she said.

"No," his smile faded. "You are too mature for that. Your mother said you were very mature, and I can see it for myself now." He spoke seriously, but Phoebe sensed a hint of mockery in his seriousness.

"What did you come for?" she asked.

"Ah, yes," he inclined his head to her. "I must get down to business. I came first to deliver this packet of tea to your mother. She told me last night that she had never tasted Japanese green tea, and I want her to try it. I heard footsteps here and thought she might have come home." He smiled again. "I also came to tell her, and perhaps you will do it for me, that I will come to call for you both at half-past six, if that is convenient. I have made a reservation for seven."

Phoebe stared at him and said nothing because she hadn't any idea what he was talking about.

"Everything I say seems to offend you," he complained. "If you will tell me why, perhaps I can do something about it." Again he inclined his head.

"I — I just don't understand," faltered Phoebe, feeling stupid.

"I'm taking you and your mother out to dinner tonight, at the Mottrell Arms. For a country inn, it's quite nice. Didn't she tell you?"

Phoebe shook her head. "I've already bought two pork chops for supper."

"Oh dear," Mr. Tarlton clucked with his tongue. "I'm sure she intended to tell you because I did specially ask you too, and she said she thought that if you hadn't too much homework, you would like to come. Won't the pork chops keep?"

A terrible black suspicion that Miranda didn't want her to come was creeping into Phoebe's heart. "She never told me," she said.

"It must have slipped her mind. You know what a terrible schedule she has. Miss Dwight keeps her on the run so that she hardly has a moment to call her own."

So, thought Phoebe, she complained about Miss Dwight and her schedule to him as if he were an old friend, even though she's told me lots of times never to tell anyone that Miss Dwight is a slave driver because it might get back to her, and then Miranda would be in trouble.

"I am sure that Miranda — ah Mrs. Smith — wants you to come along. We both do."

He calls her Miranda, Phoebe's thoughts raced on. He says "we" as if they were old buddies, and she made a date with him and never told me that I was invited too.

Phoebe looked Mr. Tarlton all over, trying to see what was so great about him. He was certainly well dressed, from his pink, button-down shirt collar all the way down to his shiny, oxblood loafers, but he wasn't handsome the way Phil had been, and although the egg-head glasses gave his eyes a harmless, owlish look, they didn't fool Phoebe. She knew the ice was there. Didn't

Miranda know it too? How could Miranda, for whom Phoebe had brushed off so many flames, now brush off Phoebe herself for a stuck-up Tarlton? There he stood, bold as brass inside the door, still holding his parcel, smiling and making apologies for Miranda as if he owned her.

"Of course, we don't want to twist your arm. You don't have to come with us, but we will be very happy to have you."

There were the "we's" again, and Phoebe was sure that his icy Tarlton eyes were condescending behind his glasses, and he was being kind and polite and asking Phoebe to go along because she was so feeble that it didn't matter to him if she went along or not. Smiling and looking distinguished, he was just the sort Miranda would fall for. She was distinguished herself, and she would appreciate Japanese paintings and Japanese tea, and she would never guess that, beneath that stylish shirt, his heart was as cold as his eyes were behind their glasses.

Anyway, Miranda had no business brushing off her only child this way, and he had no business taking her out, and Phoebe wasn't so feeble that she was letting them get away with it — cold, cruel, heartless betrayers both! Tears sprang to her eyes. She glared at Mr. Tarlton through the tears and noted with satisfaction that now he looked blurred and hideous.

"I wouldn't go anywhere with you, thank you, not if you paid me a million dollars," she said, and, placing both fists on his chest, she pushed him out the door. She shut the door after him and locked it, then stood stock still. A wild exhilaration, unlike anything she had ever felt before, flamed up inside her. With one shove she had toppled Mr. Stuck-up Tarlton right out the door and down the stairs. It was easy as pie. The fierce joy swelled inside, soared up like a rocket. It served him right! It served them all right, and it served Miranda right most of all!

As suddenly as she had soared, Phoebe fizzled out. She was shaking all over. New tears sprang to her eyes. "Oh, Miranda!" she sobbed, and turning to the wall, she leaned her head against it and cried like a baby.

A hollow bong resounded out of the abyss of the stairwell and startled Phoebe so that she stopped crying. Miss Tarlton's grandfather clock down in the first-floor hall bonged five times, wheezed as if it were clearing its sinuses, and fell silent. Phoebe groaned. Miranda would be home in half an hour, and then Miss Tarlton, bonging and wheezing like her clock, would come to tell them to leave at once because of what Phoebe had done. Assault and battery was what she thought it was called. Mr. Tarlton would have told his aunt all about it, and no one, not even Phoebe herself, could expect Miss Tarlton to keep a wild girl in her house who assaulted and battered visitors and shoved them down the stairs. Phoebe could never explain or excuse her behavior to Miss Tarlton, much less to Miranda. She didn't want to try. She just wanted to get away from all of it — ski lessons skipped or unskipped, math tests, compositions, Denby School and all the girls who went there, and the whole town of Denby too. Miranda would hardly miss her. She had her work and her new friend.

Phoebe stifled a sob. She knew what she had to do. It was risky and scary, but she wasn't so feeble as they thought. She had to back the Goldfinch out of the garage before Miranda got home and drive in it back to Charlotte and Rags in Putnam Park. Charlotte would be surprised, but not angry, and she could explain to Charlotte better than she could to Miranda. Charlotte would let her stay, and maybe Miranda would visit them once in a while. It wouldn't be like the old happy days, but it would be better than this.

She felt her way along the wall to the light switch and snapped it on. The keys to the Goldfinch were in their usual place in the dish on the hall table. She hurried to her bedroom, turned on the lights, grabbed a Kleenex, gave her nose a few good blows, fished her suitcase out of the closet, stuffed into it as many clothes as she could, added her money, and forced the lid shut. She dragged the suitcase into the hall, set it down to put on her coat, couldn't find the coat, and remembered that she had left it in the Eagle's Nest, along with the plugged-in heater and her library book.

She had the door to the Eagle's Nest unlocked and was up the stairs in a minute. The heater glowed bright red and cast a red glare on the wall opposite it. The Eagle's Nest was almost too hot. Phoebe lingered just for a minute to look out for the last time at Old Mott's big black hump silhouetted against the last light in the sky. Her Eagle's Nest was the only thing she would miss, and it wasn't hers. Nothing in Denby was, not even Miranda anymore. She unplugged the heater, lifted it carefully by the handle because it was so hot, scooped up the book

37

and the coat, went down the stairs, locked the door, remembered, rather cleverly she thought, to put the key back into the jar on the mantel, replaced the heater in the bathroom, and was ready to go. In the hall, as she put on her coat, it occurred to her that Miranda would have to return the library book for her. She saw Miranda entering the library.

"Whatever has become of my friend, Phoebe?" asked Miss Hawkins. "She used to take out so many books, but she never comes here anymore, and I miss her."

And what did Miranda do? She burst out crying right in the middle of the library.

"I miss her too," she sobbed, "more than you can ever know, for I am her mother, and I drove her away, and I shall never be happy again."

Once more tears were streaming down Phoebe's cheeks. There was one more thing she had to do. She tore a sheet from her school notebook, rummaged out a pencil, and wrote:

DEAR MIRANDA:
I AM GOING HOME. PLEASE RETURN MY LIBRARY BOOK BEFORE IT IS DUE.

She paused a minute and let her tears splash on the paper, then she wrote on:

MR. TARLTON WILL CALL FOR YOU AT 6:30. I HOPE YOU ENJOY YOUR DINNER WITH HIM.

LOVE,
PHOEBE

She laid the library book and the note on the hall table where Miranda would be sure to see them, wiped her eyes, gave her nose another blow, put on her cap, mittens, and overshoes, snatched up the keys and the suitcase, and departed down the backstairs.

[7]

PHOEBE GOT TO THE GARAGE and opened the doors without anyone's trying to stop her. The good old Goldfinch started at the first try. She backed it jerkily, but successfully, out into the street, came about, and headed toward the intersection with Mountain Road. As soon as she was out of sight of the house, she turned on her headlights, and, although her heart thumped and her hands trembled, she accomplished the turn into Mountain Road without a hitch. Half a mile ahead, Mountain Road joined Main Street; then came the town green, the town hall and the library on the right, and, on the left, the post office and some stores. The main road between Paxton and Boston crossed Main Street here. In the middle of the intersection, which was bright as day under an arc light, Mr. Wade stood inside his white circle, directing traffic. It burst upon Phoebe that, to make the left turn onto the Boston Road (scary enough by itself), she would have to swing the car right around Mr. Wade and through his pool of light, and he would surely recognize the Goldfinch (many a time she had waved to him when she drove by with Miranda), see that Phoebe, not Miranda, was driving, and stop her, because he knew perfectly well that she was too young to have a license.

Phoebe's heart seemed to stop. Her stomach twitched and writhed. She thought she might throw up. She put on the brake and tried to think of a way out. A car honked at her from behind, then passed. Another car honked; this driver shouted something at her as he passed. Phoebe took her foot off the brake. As the Goldfinch rolled on toward the intersection, Phoebe remembered just in the nick of time, the alley behind the post office. It was one way — she couldn't remember which way — but if she could turn left into it, it would take her around Mr. Wade and the intersection and deposit her on the main road to Boston, south of the town. She looked in the mirror. Nothing was coming from behind. Ahead the road was clear. She took a deep breath, shifted to low, turned the Goldfinch sharply and drove right across Main Street. In the sweep of her headlights she saw the arrow at the end of the alley pointing, thank heavens, her way. She shifted up and stepped on the gas; as she turned the wheel to straighten it, a pair of enormous, blinding headlights rushed out of the black mouth of the alley straight at the Goldfinch and crashed into it. The Goldfinch recoiled, shuddered, stalled, and stopped. Phoebe lurched into the steering wheel. Ahead everything went black. She heard the tinkling of broken glass, then the grating of hinges as the door of the other car opened. A towering figure took shape in the darkness. Either from shock or plain fright, Phoebe fainted. The next thing she knew she was still slumped against the steering wheel, but a flashlight was playing over her, and two voices were talking. She kept very still and listened.

"Do you know this kid?" asked one voice.

"It's Phoebe Smith," said the other voice, which she recognized as Mr. Wade's.

"She's a nice kid, a quiet kid that reads a lot. I wouldn't expect her to get into an accident like this. I wish she'd come to." Someone, she guessed it was Mr. Wade, took her wrist and felt her pulse.

"All kids seem to be rotten these days," said the other voice. "Those kids I'm supposed to keep track of are driving me bananas. You understand, don't you, Wade, that if they weren't driving me bananas, I wouldn't be driving down a one-way street the wrong way?" There was a pause. "Well, how is she? It would be just my luck if she was crippled or dead."

"Her pulse is steady," said Mr. Wade. "I don't think she's badly hurt, just dazed."

"Poor kid," said the other, "I suppose she has troubles too, or she wouldn't be running away, and from the look of the suitcase, that's what she was doing. I ought to feel sorry for her, but those devils have drained all the milk of human kindness right out of me. You do understand, Wade, don't you?"

"I understand, Purdy," said Mr. Wade. "Just calm down."

"I hate this lousy job," Purdy went on. "I don't like the old man any better than I like his kids, but the pay's good, and jobs don't come easy at my age, and if I'm fired for a stupid mistake like this, I'm washed up."

"I'll do all I can for you with Mr. Mottrell," said Mr. Wade. "Maybe he won't fire you." Phoebe felt him stroke her forehead. "Hi, Phoebe, are you feeling better?"

41

Phoebe opened her eyes and lifted her head. A police car drove up and trained its searchlight on them.

"Is the Goldfinch, I mean is the car hurt?"

"Nothing serious. The headlights are broken, and there's a dent in the fender," said Mr. Wade. "What about you? Do you hurt anywhere?"

"No," said Phoebe, "I'm all right."

"That's the important thing," replied Mr. Wade.

"What are you going to do to me?"

Mr. Wade patted her shoulder. "Nothing to worry about. First, as soon as you feel like standing up, I'll ask you to move into the police car, so we can get the bumpers of your car and Purdy's unlocked and the tow trucks can haul them to the garage; then someone will drive you home so you can talk the whole business over with your parents."

"I only have a mother," said Phoebe, and, as if summoned, Miranda dashed in out of the darkness. She pushed past Mr. Wade and Mr. Purdy, threw herself at Phoebe, hugged her, kissed her, and begged her, between sobs, to say she wasn't hurt.

"I'm all right, Miranda. I did an awful thing, and I'm sorry."

"Don't *you* be sorry, dear. It was all *my* fault."

They clung together, awkwardly because of the steering wheel and the suitcase, until Mr. Wade removed the suitcase and escorted them to the police car.

Mr. Charles Tarlton appeared. He seemed as con-concerned about Phoebe as Mr. Wade and Miranda herself. He didn't mention assault or battery or punishment, or even demand an apology. Phoebe was too dazed to understand what he said about one-hundred-dollar deductibles and no charges pressed, but it all seemed part of the mystifying grownup insistence that Phoebe shouldn't worry, even though she knew she had done unforgivable things, and she knew everyone else knew too. Mr. Tarlton disappeared as suddenly as he appeared. The tow truck arrived. It backed and filled and roared, and its headlights cut yellow swaths in the darkness. Phoebe snuggled close to Miranda in the police car. She wondered if perhaps she was still unconscious, and she sat very still and tried to stay unconscious because she was afraid that if she woke up it would be in a hospital, or, more likely, in jail.

At Miranda's request, the driver of the police car dropped them at their corner, so Miss Tarlton wouldn't see the car and want to know what had happened. As soon as she got inside the apartment, Phoebe knew for sure that she was wide awake and in her senses. It was cold and cheerless as ever and exactly the way she had left it. Still Miranda didn't turn on her either in reproach or in anger.

Indeed, Miranda seemed to think of nothing but Phoebe's comfort and happiness. She brought up the firewood herself and laid a fire in the parlor fireplace, so they could eat supper cosily in front of it. While Phoebe sat idle by the fire, Miranda not only set the table, but also brought out two wineglasses and the bottle of sherry she kept for special occasions. She filled Phoebe's glass and told her to sip at it while the pork chops fried. Phoebe did. The fire flickered warm on her legs, and gradually a warm glow suffused all her insides.

Miranda served up the pork chops. She hovered over Phoebe and helped her to applesauce. Phoebe's burden of guilt, which all the grownup admonitions not to worry hadn't lightened, slipped away. She sipped her wine and chewed her chop. She had never in her life felt more carefree. As if one of the new television sets had been brought into the room especially for her, she saw the events of the afternoon playing themselves out before her eyes. No movie she had ever seen had been more absorbing or exciting than her own wonderful adventures. She longed to know about the parts she had missed.

"Why didn't you tell me we'd been invited out to dinner before I bought the pork chops?" she asked.

Miranda, sitting opposite, her eyes full of love, said, "In the morning, dear, I was so rushed it went clean out of my head. I remembered later, but I hadn't a minute to find you and tell you. In the afternoon, when I saw the buses coming back from the ski slopes, I dashed out of a class to catch you and tell you before you started home, but you weren't on either of the buses. I asked the gym teacher about you. She was very cross. She said you'd skipped ski class without an excuse and she was going to report you. I said I was sure you had just gone home because you were sick."

"I had skipped," said Phoebe, feeling neither remorse nor fear.

"Don't worry, dear," said Miranda. "I had to go back to my class. Then I had a meeting. I rushed home as soon as I could and I found your note."

"What did you do?"

"I didn't know what to do. I'd known that you

were lonely here and not very happy, but I never dreamed you'd desert me, Phoebe. I thought we'd weather it out together until things got better, and we had our own home here with Charlotte." Miranda's voice trembled. Her eyes looked misty, perhaps with tears. Phoebe felt sorry for her.

"You see, Miranda, I thought you hadn't told me on purpose because you wanted to go out with Mr. Tarlton without me."

Miranda shook her head, "I would never do that, but it's just what Charles said you thought. He is very perceptive."

"Did he say anything about what I did to him?"

Miranda was misty all over now, and her reply seemed a little misty and beside the point too.

"I was standing in the hall, still holding your note, worried to death because I knew you had taken the Goldfinch. I couldn't decide what to do. I didn't want to telephone Charlotte or the police from the house because of Miss Tarlton. I'd just about decided to go out to a phone booth, when Charles knocked and came in. I told him all about it. He said we must get right into his car and go after you because he'd talked to you, and you were upset, and we should try to catch you and explain to you as soon as we could."

"But what did he say about what I did?"

"Nothing. We set right out after you, and we'd no sooner turned onto Mountain Road than we saw the accident ahead, and I had a feeling, and then, oh, Phoebe, I recognized the Goldfinch, and I made Charles stop, and I jumped out and ran over to it, and when I found that you weren't hurt, I was so grateful and happy that nothing else mattered, and nothing else does matter, except that you are safe." Miranda's face, pink and blurry around the edges, swayed back and forth before Phoebe's eyes, like a big flower on its stalk.

"Didn't he tell you that I yelled at him and shoved him down the stairs?"

"No, and I'm sure you didn't."

"Yes, I did." Phoebe tried to focus her eyes on Miranda until she came clear, but it was too hard and she gave up.

"He knew you were upset. He wouldn't hold anything you said or did against you. He is very understanding and kind."

Now Miranda's blurred flower face hovered just above Phoebe, and her hands reached out like graceful tendrils, but before she surrendered herself to this blurred and blissful embrace, Phoebe had to make one thing clear.

"I love you, Miranda," she said with an effort because her tongue didn't want to move, "but, just the same, I don't like Mr. Tarlton."

[8]

PHOEBE WOKE UP next morning with a dry mouth and a headache. The events of the day before passed through her mind, right up to eating the pork chop. Then everything went blank. Yet here she was in her nightgown, in her bed, between the sheets, with the quilt tucked around her, and her school clothes laid out on the chair. She had little time to wonder about this. Miranda popped her head in the door to say it was seven-thirty.

Obedient to habit, Phoebe kicked off the covers and leaped out of bed. It was like jumping into the Bering Sea. She snatched up her clothes and dashed for the comparative warmth of the bathroom. She was trying to wash away the headache with dabs of water when Miranda popped in again to say that she was leaving early to do some work before school started, that she had left the grocery list and five dollars on the kitchen counter, that Phoebe must remember to unplug the heater, and she must hurry, but not worry. Miranda kissed her and was gone.

The sharp morning air, along with the exertion of stashing away the grocery list and the money in her zipper pocket while she held on to her books, ate a piece of toast, and ran to school, cleared Phoebe's head enough so that she remembered the math test just in time to take it. It was a disaster. She consoled herself by devoting her study period to the writing of a composition called *Why I Hate Skiing*. She minced no words. After all, Miss Parsons had asked for it. As she handed in her effort at the beginning of English class, she felt bold and defiant, but a test on punctuation deflated her. In French class she was so obviously unprepared that the teacher pretended she wasn't there. For the first time, she had a moment to assess her situation.

Yesterday she had gone on a regular rampage, as

47

Charlotte would call it, and what had it got her? Charlotte and home were as far away as ever. The Goldfinch was smashed, while Miss Tarlton and her abominable nephew were still there, and still threatening. School was the same old misery and promised to get worse, what with the skipped ski class, the flunked math, and the smart-aleck composition. Her head began to ache again. When the bell rang for the end of class, Phoebe longed to lay it on her desk and go to sleep, but that would just make more trouble. She dragged herself and her books out into the corridor, where the stream of girls caught her up and carried her along toward the lunchroom. She tried to ignore the shouted greetings, laughter, waving hands, pokes, and shoves going on around her. She knew they were not for her. She particularly ignored a voice that seemed to be calling, "Phoebe." She knew that if anyone was calling her, which was unlikely, it wouldn't be "Phoebe" they'd be calling, but "Feeble."

"Phoebe!" The voice was right in her ear. "Will you eat lunch with me? I want to talk to you." Phoebe saw Constance Mottrell looking down at her and smiling. "Will you?"

"Y-yes, if you really want."

"Good. Here, take the books and grab that little table in the corner. I'll go get the food. Do you want anything special?"

Phoebe shook her head.

"Then I might as well get the hot lunch for us both." Constance unloaded her books into Phoebe's arms and worked her way toward the line forming along the counter.

Phoebe made straight for the table in the corner, dropped the books on it and sat down. She felt dizzy.

Of all the rich girls in that school, Constance Mottrell was certainly the richest. No one else came and left each day in a Rolls Royce, which, for all it looked so old-fashioned, was, as Phoebe had learned from Ben, the cream of motor cars. But riches weren't the half of it. Of all the accomplished and remote girls in the school, Constance was the most accomplished and the remotest. Dignity and gravity wrapped her around, set her apart, and raised her as high above the others as they rose above Phoebe herself. Though Constance was good at studies, she never showed off by comparing grades. Though she played well all the games that mattered, she never shrieked or moaned or stamped when she lost, or explained modestly that she had just been lucky when she won. She never wore make-up, or fiddled with her hair in the washroom. She never giggled, or squealed, or whispered secrets. Though everyone respected her, she hadn't a best friend. She was, so it seemed to Phoebe, like a princess, enchanted or in disguise, who was passing some time at Denby School for Girls, but whose real life was in another, higher sphere.

Phoebe rubbed her eyes and forehead and watched Constance proceed along the food line. Taller than most, with her blonde hair in an unfashionable braid down her back, carelessly dressed in clothes that the cute girls wouldn't wear to a dog fight, she still was fairest of them all — a princess among clods. It was unthinkable that she should have asked Phoebe to eat lunch with her, and Phoebe wondered if she was having hallucinations along with the headache. She rubbed her eyes again. Constance was coming toward her with a loaded tray and calling out for her to dump the books onto the floor so she could set the tray on the table.

"They call it tuna casserole," said Constance as she unloaded the tray, "but everything here tastes just like everything else, so I can't swear to it." She tried a mouthful of casserole and shrugged. "When you're hungry, everything tastes O.K."

Phoebe watched her eat in silence. The wonder of being so close to Constance had robbed her of both appetite and speech. Constance polished off the casserole, made some jabs at her salad, and finished her milk before she sat back and gave Phoebe a long look.

"I'd never have guessed you had it in you!"

"Had what in me?" Phoebe managed to say.

"Guts," replied Constance, "the guts to steal a car and run away in it."

Phoebe felt as if the breath had been knocked out of her. She had to gasp a few times before she could say anything.

"How . . . ?" she finally managed to say. "How do you know?"

"I saw you go barreling into the Fossil and Old Gestapo. I saw the whole thing. It was absolutely terrific."

"I hit a car, but . . . , but . . ."

"You hit the Fossil. That's what we call the Rolls because it looks like one, and anyway it makes them all mad, and the reason you hit it was because Gestapo — that's what we call Purdy the chauffeur, because he's a spy — was driving down the one-way alley the wrong way. So it was all his fault." A bold, devil-may-care spark glinted in Constance's usually grave blue eyes. She grinned.

Phoebe remembered Purdy. "Were you in the Rolls — er, Fossil?"

"Nope." Constances grin got wickeder. She was looking more like a girl pirate than a princess. "The Gestapo was chasing me in the Fossil. I ran down the alley the wrong way on purpose. He followed me. He almost had me. I ducked behind a trash can, and you came charging in and zapped him." Constance laughed aloud, showing a set of very even white and, it seemed to Phoebe, sharp teeth.

"Harry and I are sorry you didn't get to run away. We know what it's like to want to, but if you had, the Fossil wouldn't have got zapped, and we'd never have known about you. Harry wants to see you."

Phoebe felt as if she had herself been zapped.

"It's not just because of what you did to the Fossil," Constance went on. Her eyes glinted. "You're the one who has *Tiger of the Snows* out for a month, and you had *The Conquest of Everest,* and *Nanga Parabat, The Killer Mountain,* and now you've got *Alone to Everest.* Miss Hawkins told me when I asked for it yesterday afternoon because Harry had just heard about it, and Miss Hawkins told me she'd saved it for you because she thought you'd like it, and then she told me how you'd read all those other books too. You're librarian's pet. The only book you didn't get was *Anapurna.*"

"I've been trying to, but it's never in."

"That's because Harry and I take it out by turns, so no one else can get it. Maurice Herzog is our favorite climber."

"Tenzing Norkay is mine, and I've wanted *The Ascent of Nanda Devi* for a long time because Tenzing climbed around there before he got famous, but it's always out too."

"Harry's got that one. Some day we want to climb it. He'll probably let you have it, if you'll let him have *Alone to Everest*."

"O.K." Phoebe felt herself on firmer ground, and, getting up her courage, asked, "Who's Harry?"

"Don't you know?" Constance scowled, then shrugged. "I guess you wouldn't. I don't talk about him here because they're all twirps in this school. He's my brother. We're twins. He's got asthma, and he's had pneumonia four times, so the Hostile Powers don't let him out in winter. They have tutors come to the house to teach him. He's way ahead of me in school work, but it's dull for him having to stay in, so we read about mountain climbers and travelers in Nepal and Sikkim and Tibet. The Hostile Powers can't stop us from doing that." Constance tossed her head, and her eyes flashed.

"The Hostile Powers?" ventured Phoebe.

"The parents," explained Constance, "but never mind them. Harry and I made something this winter — it's what we needed the books for — so Harry wants me to bring you this afternoon, so you can see what we made and Harry can see you."

"What did you make?"

"Wait and see. You can come, can't you? Gestapo will drive you home."

"I — I guess so."

"Do you have to ask your mother?"

"No, but I have to buy groceries, and I have to be home by half-past five to start supper."

"That's O.K. Gestapo can let you off at the store."

The bell rang. Constance finished off her chocolate pudding. "I'll meet you in the coatroom after school." She gathered up her books and was off.

Phoebe downed her milk, wolfed a roll, and hurried after Constance. She felt excited and happy as she hadn't since coming to Denby, and her headache was gone.

[9]

THE ROLLS ROYCE with the chauffeur in attendance was waiting when Phoebe and Constance came out of school. Constance nudged Phoebe.

"Watch me get a rise out of Gestapo." She raised her voice and called, "I see you got your old Fossil fixed. I wish you'd totaled it."

"It takes more than a bump to total a car like this, Miss Constance," replied the chauffeur.

Phoebe recognized the voice as that of Purdy. As she came closer, he said, "Isn't that the girl named Phoebe Smith that ran into me yesterday?"

Constance hooted. "She didn't run into you. You ran into her. You were the one that was going the wrong way."

Purdy caught Constance's eye and held it. "You think I don't know where you went yesterday, or why you were running down that alley the wrong way. I do know, Miss Constance, and I had a talk with your father this morning, and now he knows, and he'll have a talk with you tonight." Purdy continued to hold Constance's eye.

Constance tossed her head. "I'm not afraid."

"You're not to be trusted. That's what you're not," returned Purdy, "and from now on, it's no stopping in town for anything, unless I go with you. That's Mr. Mottrell's orders." Purdy opened the rear door of the Rolls and motioned to Constance to climb in.

She glowered at him. "Phoebe's coming home with me, and you're to take her back to her house by five-thirty and stop on the way so she can buy groceries, so you'd better be waiting with the car at five."

"Very good, Miss Constance," replied Purdy, "and if you know what's good for you, you'll cut out the fresh talk and mind your manners. Now hop in."

Phoebe followed Constance into the Rolls, and Purdy slammed the door. The inside of the Rolls was upholstered in pearl gray. The seat was soft and bouncy and as they proceeded silently through town, Phoebe felt that she was being wafted on a cloud. However, she could not really enjoy her first ride in a Rolls Royce. The encounter between Constance and Purdy had left her puzzled and a little frightened. Constance sat beside her and scowled straight ahead through the glass screen at the back of Purdy's neck. She made no attempt to explain anything. Indeed she seemed to have gone into a sort of angry trance and forgotten that Phoebe was beside her. A few miles beyond town, they turned up a drive and Phoebe saw the summit of Old Mott rising, full ahead. The drive wound its way upward between clumps of snow-covered bushes and fields of snow. At intervals, Phoebe caught glimpses of a very large stone-and-brick building, bulging with bays and balconies, thrusting a jumble of gables, towers, domes, and turrets up toward the crags of Old Mott and the sombre sky. The building reminded Phoebe of the library at Miranda's college. She couldn't believe it was a house that people lived in, but the Rolls stopped under a sort of bridge that jutted out from the building over the driveway, and Constance came to.

"Here we are," she said. "We'll go see Ida first, and then we'll go up to Harry in the dumbwaiter. Come on."

Phoebe followed her up a flight of stone steps, through a huge double door, and into a foyer so vast that she could barely make out a wide stairway at the far end that rose out of the shadow, divided in two, and disappeared into shadow again. Constance cut diagonally across the foyer, and, as Phoebe followed her, her feet sank into carpeting that felt softer than Charlotte's finest velvet. Constance opened a small door in the paneling. They made their way through a maze of passages, left their books and outdoor clothes in a closet, and finally came out in a kitchen that was almost as vast as the foyer. One corner was fixed up as a sort of sitting room, with a table, a couch, and some easy chairs; and here, under a lighted lamp, a little old lady sat and sewed.

"Hi, Ida!" shouted Constance in loud, but this time friendly, tones. "I'm home, and I've brought a friend."

The little old lady dropped her sewing and jumped up. She was dressed in a starched white uniform and apron, and as she trotted toward them, she talked and gestured with such vivacity that her rosy old face was all a-twitch, and her uniform and apron crackled. She hugged Constance. She wrung Phoebe's hand and patted her cheek. Her bright little eyes sparkled, words spurted out of her, and Phoebe couldn't understand a single one of them.

Laughing, Constance said, "Just say you're glad to see her, and say it loud because she's pretty deaf. She'll understand. She thinks she's talking English, but it's so mixed up with Finnish that no one can understand her except us."

Phoebe did as she was told, and Ida responded with a burst of incomprehensible sounds.

"She's made her special coffee cake with raisins and almonds, and ginger cookies, and she'll make the coffee now and send it up," translated Constance. "Pat your stomach and say 'yum yum.' She'll like that."

"Yum yum," said Phoebe and patted her stomach.

Ida laughed like anything and went on chuckling "yum yum" to herself while she darted around the kitchen rattling the coffee pot and the crockery.

Constance went to what looked like a cupboard in the wall and opened the door. Inside was a box with shelves and a rope hanging beside it. Constance grabbed the box and rattled it, and it swung around inside the cupboard.

"It's hanging on a rope on a pulley. If you pull the rope beside it, it goes up the shaft," she explained. "I'll go up first, and you pull me, and if you get tired or anything, just call Ida. She'll understand that. She'll help you. She's O.K. She's from the old days." She stuck her head inside the box and shouted something. A faint cry answered.

"O.K.," she said and climbed into the lower half of the box. With her head bent down and her knees tucked under her chin, she just fit under the shelf.

"Now pull," she told Phoebe, shoving the rope out to her, "until you hear the box bump against the top and you can't pull any more, then wait till I yell down 'O.K.,' then play out the rope until the box comes down again, then climb in. Ida will help you, and she'll pull you up. You dig?"

"Not really," said Phoebe. "What is it?"

"It's the dumbwaiter, of course. It's meant to haul food and towels and things up to the top floor, but we use it for ourselves. We're not supposed to, but it's more fun than the stairs, and Ida doesn't mind. Come on, pull."

Phoebe gave the rope a tug, and Constance and the box lurched upward.

"Don't pull so hard, just steady!" shouted Constance, and she jerked out of sight.

Phoebe pulled and pulled, while Ida bustled around

and shouted what Phoebe guessed were words of encouragement. At last the box did bump against something way up, and the rope no longer gave to her pulls.

"O.K.," Constance's voice floated faintly down.

The rope began to slide through Phoebe's hands, and she played it out until the box bumped down in front of her. She had no time to gather her wits or her courage before consigning herself to the dumbwaiter. Ida pounced on her, bundled her into the box, folded her up, scrunched her down, arranged her hands and elbows so they wouldn't scrape, and finally shouted what sounded like "Heavahohup!" into the shaft. From afar, Constance answered. Ida directed another incomprehensible torrent of words at Phoebe, nodded, smiled, patted Phoebe's leg, grabbed the rope with both hands, and, with another "Heavahohup!" sent Phoebe shooting into darkness.

To her surprise, she wasn't frightened. The blackness and the smooth motion were so soothing that, in spite of being scrunched, she rather wished they would go on for a long time, so that she might rest before more strange things happened to her. However, she soon heard Constance, faint but understandable, telling someone about her set-to with Purdy. A deeper, husky voice answered her. Constance's voice grew louder and shriller.

"We can't let them. We've got to do something, quick!"

"Keep your shirt on," replied the husky voice. "Don't say anything now. Wait till I tell you."

[10]

THE TOP of the dumbwaiter bumped the top of the shaft. Phoebe faced an oblong of light. She climbed out, stretched, blinked, and looked about. She was in a very large attic with sloping roof and dormer windows. It seemed to be a bedroom, sitting room, playroom, and study, all in one; and in the middle of it, on a table under a lighted lamp, was what she recognized at once as a large and magnificent model of Mount Everest. There it was, rising up out of the glaciers, cwms, cols, ridges, and spurs she knew so well, with its attendant peaks of Lhotse, Nuptse, and North Peak all in their places around it. She was so entranced that it was several minutes before she noticed the boy standing beside the model.

"I'm Harry," he said with a smile, "and I guess you're Phoebe Smith, the Everest nut that zapped the Fossil. Welcome to Base Camp. We are proud to have you here." He made a little mock bow.

In a way, he looked like Constance, but he was sallow and skinny and a little stoop-shouldered; and his features, instead of being bold and regular, were all slightly askew. His smile, however, had a gay glancing quality, like sunshine. His eyes, as he looked Phoebe over, sparkled with laughter, and, she thought, friendliness. It flashed into her mind that, if Constance was a princess in disguise, Harry was a prince transformed into a charming goblin.

"People are always surprised when they see me, after they've seen Con," he said, as if he were reading Phoebe's thoughts. "She got the looks, but I got the brains." He smiled his glancing smile, and his eyes were both mocking and merry. "Along with the brains, I got the asthma — which is why they keep me up here out of the damp and dust. When I can't go out in winter, I'd as soon be up here as anywhere. I don't have to see much of the Hostile Powers, my tutors are good eggs, and Con comes up after school, and we made this." He indicated the model with a flourish. "I wanted you to see it."

Phoebe stepped closer to admire it. "It's beautiful. It's terrific. I would never have thought of making such a thing. I don't see how you did it."

"I'll explain, if you want. It'll be a while before Ida sends up the food."

"I do want," said Phoebe. "Please do."

Harry took on a serious, professional air. First he had calculated heights and distances as well as he could from his maps and had made scale drawings of the mountain from all four points of the compass. Ida had mixed a concoction of flour, salt, and water, and, guided by the scale drawings and pictures from various books, they had shaped Ida's dough into the Everest massif. They had left most of the dough, which hardened into a kind of plaster, white, like snow, but they had painted the two glaciers, the Rongbuk and the Khumbu, blue, they had splotched the lower slopes and the upper faces with gray to look like bare rock, and they had painted the Yellow Band on the North Pyramid face. It was very beautiful and realistic. Harry beckoned Phoebe to look more closely. Thin lines of different colors traced the routes of all the major Everest expeditions as high up the slopes as they had gone. Little flags of different-colored scraps of cloth glued to matchsticks were planted here and there on the sides of the mountain. These, Harry explained, marked achievements and disasters.

Here, on May 25, 1922, at 25,500 feet, on the Northeast Ridge of the Summit Pyramid, George Finch, Geoffrey Bruce, and the Ghurka Tejbir had held down their tent through a terrible blizzard which lasted all the night and on into the afternoon of the next day. Six Sherpas had brought them up beef broth and tea from the camp at the North Col, then hurried down again so as not to be overtaken by darkness. Finch, Bruce, and Tejbir spent another night in their tent and survived the cold and the altitude, they believed, because they took oxygen. The next morning, Finch and Bruce climbed to 27,235 feet, a new record, and would probably have reached the top, if Bruce's oxygen had not cut out.

Below, on the North Col, on June 7, 1922, an avalanche killed seven Sherpas.

Just below the First Step, on the Northeast Summit Ridge, Mallory and Irvine were last seen alive, on June 7, 1924.

At the foot of the same First Step, an ice axe belonging to either Mallory or Irvine was found by Wyn Harris, on May 29, 1934.

On the other side of Everest, at 27,500 feet, Lambert of the Swiss Expedition and Tenzing Norkay had spent the night of May 27, 1952, on the South Pyramid Face, in a tent without mattresses, sleeping bags, or a stove, with a little food but nothing to drink except snow melted by candle flame. They had slapped each other all night to keep warm, and the next morning had climbed to 28,215 feet, another record. They had turned back because they knew they hadn't enough strength to get to the summit and down again alive.

The final flag was at 29,200 feet, on the summit, which Hillary and Tenzing had reached on May 28, 1953.

"What do you think?" asked Harry.

Phoebe had been with her heroes. It took her a minute to come back. "It's wonderful," she sighed at last. "I wish I'd thought of making it."

"Can you think of any other great achievements or disasters that I should put up flags for?"

"I'm glad you put up a flag for the night Tenzing and Lambert spent at 27,500 feet, because Tenzing says that the night and the climb the next day needed more endurance than going to the top later with Hillary. It was a disappointment to Tenzing, too, not to get to the top with Lambert. He liked him especially."

"Actually I put up the flag because they survived without using oxygen in about the same conditions that Finch, Bruce, and Tejbir did with it. It's sort of scientific."

"Why don't you put up a flag for the Abominable

Snowman prints that the Swiss scientists found beside the glacier? That was scientific."

The food had arrived with a rattle and a bump, and Constance called them to help take it out of the dumb-waiter and carry it to their table under one of the dormer windows. Suddenly Phoebe was famished, and the coffee with whipped cream, the coffee cake, and the cookies tasted as good as if she were sharing them with Tenzing on the windswept slopes of Everest. Harry and Constance urged her to eat all she could hold. Nothing made Ida happier than to have her offerings eaten up. Just outside the window, very close, Old Mott seemed to be watching them; he looked rugged, fierce, and wild, with snow blowing off his top in a plume just as if he were Everest.

Harry took up Phoebe's suggestion. "I would give the Yeti — or the Abominable Snowman as you call him — a flag, if I was sure he existed."

Constance said she was sure. She had read an article in the newspaper. The Yeti is a big ape. He can be anywhere from five to eight feet tall, and he lives in the rocky marginal forests of the Himalayas, just at the vegetation line. He eats roots and berries and twigs and moss, and small animals, birds, and insects. He usually stays hidden in the high brush, but sometimes he comes out onto the snowfields, probably to find a kind of moss he likes that only grows at very high altitudes. Then he leaves his footprints in the snow. Constance was quite certain about her information, and Phoebe had no wish to doubt her. But Harry objected that no educated westerner had ever seen a Yeti close to. Constance replied that the Yeti is very clever and very shy. He stays away from people who are looking for him. Only once in a while does he turn up near a village. Lots of natives in Sikkim, Nepal, and Kardoram have seen Yetis, but they are afraid of them and never chase them.

Phoebe told them how Tenzing's father had seen Yetis twice and heard the whistling noise they make. She suggested that maybe the Yeti is a sort of missing link, a leftover from prehistoric ages before men were separated from apes. Both Harry and Constance accepted this suggestion with respect, and Phoebe had another piece of coffee cake. She had never enjoyed a conversation more.

Harry said there were strange things hidden among the vast empty spaces at the top of the world, and strange happenings that couldn't always be explained by science; and he told about something that had happened on Everest that Phoebe, for all her reading, had never known before. In 1934, two days after the ice axe of Mallory or Irvine was found on the Northeast Ridge, F. S. Smythe was climbing there alone, Shipton his companion having turned back. From the moment that Shipton turned back, Smythe felt very strongly that another friendly companion was just behind him, roped to him, watching out for him. He was so certain of the friend behind him that, when he stopped to eat, he reached back to hand him some of his cake. It wasn't until he was almost in sight of camp again that the feeling of having a companion left him. Then, while he was approaching the camp, he saw two black things like kites or balloons hovering in the sky over the Northeast Ridge. They pulsed like hearts. Smythe was afraid he was having hallucinations. He tested himself by looking away, identifying peaks and glaciers, and then looking back at the two pulsing, flying things. They were still there. One had squat wings; the other had a beak like a teakettle. They hovered in the sky until a cloud blew over them and hid them from Smythe's sight.

Smiling thoughtfully, his eyes resting on Phoebe, Harry went on to ask whether some peculiar physical condition — brought on perhaps by the altitude or by fatigue — enabled Smythe to notice things men don't ordinarily notice, even though they are there. Or was there a spirit that lived on the mountain as the Sherpas believed? Or were the spirits of Mallory and Irvine wandering near the place where they had died? Was one or were both of them watching over Smythe? Perhaps they had reached the summit before they died, and they wanted to tell Smythe, but couldn't penetrate through his human consciousness to make him understand. He only felt their presence. And the two pulsing, black things: Were they another misunderstood attempt by the dead climbers to make themselves known, or were they birds of some hitherto unknown species? And, to get back to the Yeti, wasn't there really more evidence for his being some sort of supernatural manifestation than for his being a missing link? The natives believed he was a spirit that brought bad luck, and they had seen him, which was more than any scientific expedition had done.

Harry's words and Harry's husky voice sent shivers up and down Phoebe's spine. She remembered the dream that Tenzing had had about Thornley and Crace on Nanga Parbat, and, in hushed tones, she told it. Thornley, Crace, and Marsh were three daredevil young Englishmen who thought they could climb Nanga Parbat — the mountain that had already killed thirty men — and that they could do it alone and in winter. Their Sherpas, among them Tenzing — not yet illustrious — refused to go with them beyond Camp One. The young men, ignoring gales and bitter cold, pushed on without them. Through glasses the Sherpas watched the little black figures crawling up over the glacier and making camp a little higher each night. Marsh got such badly frozen feet that he had to come down. Thornley and Crace pushed on, and then Tenzing had his dream.

He dreamed that Thornley and Crace were coming toward him dressed in new clothes, surrounded by people without faces. Although he was not a superstitious man, Tenzing knew this was a bad omen, and the next morning when he looked for the camp of Thornley and Crace up on the glacier, it had disappeared. Marsh and the Sherpas sent out search parties, but storms drove them back. Thornley and Crace were never seen again.

In the gathering darkness, the children huddled together and spoke of the malignity of Nanga Parbat, The Naked Mountain. They spoke of the men who had died on it, sixteen of them in a single avalanche in 1937, the others more horribly, from exposure, by twos and threes. Each new expedition discovered the frozen bodies of men whom the mountain had already killed. The final conquest of Nanga Parbat by Hermann Buhl was attended by misunderstandings, ill feeling, recriminations, and a general atmosphere of gloom. Buhl behaved strangely. His companion had deserted him. There was no exultation among the climbers, only grim relief when Buhl returned half dead, though victorious.

How different was the conquest of Everest! Each of the great peaks had a spirit of its own. Everest was noble and proud, and if a spirit did inhabit it, that spirit might well have tried to speak to Smythe about the climbers who had been killed. But Nanga Parbat was sinister and cruel; its spirit hated mortal men.

The rattling of the dumbwaiter and the shouts of Ida from below must have blended into the children's fantasies like the whine of the Yeti or the grinding of the avalanche and the howling of the wind. It took Ida in person, red-faced, breathless — though not too breathless to shout in her own peculiar language — to wrench them back to reality. It seemed, as Constance translated, that Gestapo had been waiting for Phoebe for fifteen minutes. If she didn't hurry, the A&P would be closed, but that was only part of what Ida was saying.

Constance jumped up. "I told you so." She fixed her eyes on Harry. "They're back. They want to see me. Now! What do I do?"

"Keep your shirt on," said Harry, but his voice shook and cracked. The two stood rigid staring at each other.

"What's the matter?" asked Phoebe.

Harry glanced at her, then turned back to his sister. "Nothing," he said crossly.

Constance didn't even look at Phoebe. She shouted

something at Ida, who shouted back, then took Phoebe by the wrist. Phoebe said good-bye twice, loudly, but, if Constance and Harry heard her, they paid no attention. They went on staring at each other. "Is anything wrong?" ventured Phoebe. Again they didn't seem to hear.

Ida jerked Phoebe's wrist and led her down a long winding stair and through the dark passages to the closet where she had left her things. Hurriedly, but with reassuring nods and noises, Ida helped her into her outdoor clothes, piled her books in her arms, led her through more passages and back across the foyer to the front door, where Gestapo and the Fossil were waiting.

[11]

THEY JUST MADE IT to the A&P, and Miranda's list and the money were still in Phoebe's pocket. From the A&P, the Fossil whisked Phoebe to Miss Tarlton's front door. Phoebe hadn't the nerve to pull out the speaking tube and ask Gestapo to take her around to the back. He climbed out to open the car door for her and to help her lug her books and the groceries over the snowbank onto the sidewalk. After she had thanked him, he stood a minute, looking down at her.

"It's none of my business," he said, "but you seem like a decent kid. If I was you, I'd steer clear of those two. They're bad medicine."

Phoebe stared at him with her mouth open. It took

her a minute to get over her surprise enough to shake her head and say, "Oh, no."

Gestapo sighed. "You don't believe me. I didn't expect you to, but don't say I didn't warn you." He turned and climbed back over the snowbank to the road.

Phoebe stood alone in the dark. A gust of wind rattled through the bare trees and poked icy fingers right through her coat to her skin and on into her bones. Suddenly she was scared. Something was wrong. Deep down in her cold bones, she felt that Gestapo wasn't just being officious, that he really was warning her of something bad, but what? She tried to scramble up over the snowbank to call him back, but she slipped and dropped her books and the grocery bag; and when she finally made it to the top of the bank, the taillight of the Fossil was disappearing around the corner. She slid back down to the sidewalk and began to brush herself off and collect her belongings. The snow was hard and gray and gritty. It had lacerated her hands as well as chilled them. Her underpants were wet from sliding down the bank, and the cold wind wormed its way right up under her skirt and was freezing her wet underpants to her cold bottom, which she suspected was lacerated too. Above her the bare trees still rattled and sighed dismally, and the façade of Miss Tarlton's house rose up grim and gray, with one light on on the third floor. Miranda was up there in the cold, tired after work, and probably worried and cross because Phoebe was late and there was nothing to cook for supper. There'd be no fire or sherry tonight, just hamburger in the cold kitchen, and then homework.

How different everything was up in Harry's attic on

the slopes of Old Mott! Outdoors, the snow lay soft and white as swansdown. Indoors, it was warm and cozy and safe and exciting and mysterious, all at once. Even the good old Eagle's Nest was a poor thing compared to Harry's attic. The happiness of the afternoon seemed to envelop Phoebe again — the friendliness of Constance and Harry, Ida and her goodies, the wonderful model, the thrilling sound of Harry's husky voice, and, best of all, the sense of comradeship as they drew close around the table and swapped tales in the gathering dusk. How could anything be wrong among such friends, in such a place? And if anything was wrong — Phoebe hastily smothered the memory of the last few puzzling minutes of her visit — who cared? She tossed her head. She could feel her eyes flash the way Constance's did. She'd really be a twirp to let Gestapo scare her. Wasn't he an enemy and a spy? Hadn't Constance said so? Phoebe tossed her head again and marched around to the back door.

Miss Tarlton was there, sweeping out the entry. "I just saw the Mottrell's Rolls Royce stop to let you out. I suppose you have been playing with little Constance."

Phoebe felt she couldn't stand Miss Tarlton's questions or the stories that were sure to follow. She nodded and said, "Excuse me, Miss Tarlton, I must hurry upstairs. I am late, and my mother will be worried about me."

"You are a good child to think of your mother, but you needn't hurry on her account." Miss Tarlton smiled.

"I have all the food for our supper, and she is hungry," declared Phoebe, and she tried to go straight up the stairs. Miss Tarlton and her broom blocked the way.

"Pleasant company can make one forget even the pangs of hunger." Miss Tarlton's smile widened so that all her yellow upper teeth showed. "My nephew Charles went up to see your mother over an hour ago to take her a book, and I'll lay you dollars to doughnuts that he is telling her about his beloved Japan. On that subject, Charles is a regular spellbinder. Listening to him, I'm sure your mother has forgotten all about time."

Phoebe felt, as Charlotte would have said, all the starch go out of her. She propped her books against the stair rail and slumped over them. The combined Tarltons were too much for her.

"How nice that you and little Constance are chums," Miss Tarlton pressed on. "Little Constance and I are cousins, you know, thrice removed."

Phoebe wished silently that someone would remove Miss Tarlton along with her irresistible nephew, far away, forever. "Little Constance" she was certain would have felt the same way and would have said so out loud, with her head high, and her eyes flashing.

Phoebe said, "Oh."

"I suppose you saw Harry too. How is he?"

"Fine."

"Really!" Miss Tarlton bared her teeth again and threw back her head so she looked like a startled horse. "I'm so glad. I had heard differently. Several close calls this winter — touch and go — saved by a miracle drug. Of course he never will be strong. Since Big Constance — the children's mother — died, I don't get much news of the Mottrell cousins. Did the twins speak of their mother?"

Phoebe shook her head.

"Her death was a terrible loss to us all. Weak lungs, you know. It runs in her family, just as surely as the vicious streak runs in the Mottrells. Those poor children haven't a very good heritage." Miss Tarlton paused and licked her lips as if she were enjoying a quiet gloat.

"They seemed O.K. to me," replied Phoebe, a trifle defiantly.

Miss Tarlton disregarded this. "I don't suppose you saw Cousin Henry, the twins' father, or their new mother — Barbara I believe is her name?"

"No," said Phoebe.

"Too bad. I hear they are off electioneering every chance they get. Henry is dead set on being governor, and I dare say this new woman of his, this Barbara, fancies herself as the next first lady of New Hampshire." Miss Tarlton tossed her head and snorted, again rather like a horse. "I've never met her. They didn't ask me to their wedding, though they asked just about everyone else in the state. She hasn't even come to call. I guess she hasn't the breeding to know what is correct, but Henry does. I was deeply offended. Not that I'd have gone to the wedding. I hate rubbing elbows with low-class politicians, and I couldn't have endured to watch this new woman flaunting herself as mistress of Dream-wold."

"Dreamwold," repeated Phoebe. The word seemed to her to rise up out of all the mean, harsh ones like a flower from a snowbank.

"Absurd, isn't it?" exclaimed Miss Tarlton. "But that's what they call that eyesore they live in, and it's not as if they hadn't the money to tear it down and build something in good taste. The Mottrells have no taste at all, except a taste for money. Dreamwold indeed! I call it Bad Dreamwold, Nightmarewold! Ha, ha!"

Phoebe had been murmuring "Dreamwold" to herself. How well the beautiful, mysterious name suited the abode of Constance and Harry. For a moment Phoebe felt herself floating back into the afternoon's happiness.

Miss Tarlton's "Ha, ha!" broke the spell. "Did the twins mention their older brother?" she demanded.

Phoebe shook her head.

"I expect he's up to no good. Even before his poor, dear mother died, he was always into some sort of trouble. Since then, it's been far worse, so I hear." Miss Tarlton lowered her voice. "Jail, so I'm told, though Henry has done his best to hush it up. It's the vicious streak I mentioned. The Mottrells have it in the blood. Are you sure the twins didn't mention Tony? I'd be interested to know about him. His real name is Tarlton, but for some reason they called him Tony, as if he were an organ grinder. No Mottrell was ever called anything like that before, but since he's been such a disgrace, I'm glad they don't call him Tarlton. We Tarltons may not be rich, but our name is unsullied; and, of course," Miss Tarlton gave a self-satisfied smile, "we have a ghost, which is more than the Mottrells ever had!"

Harsh and shrill from the depths of the house came six bongs, followed by a wheeze. "Mercy," cried Miss Tarlton. "Charles and I are engaged to go out for dinner. We should be on our way this minute. He must really be holding forth up there." She nodded at Phoebe and stepped aside to let her pass. "Run up, like a good child, and tell him that I said we must start at once."

Phoebe found Miranda and Mr. Charles Tarlton in the parlor, drinking weak tea out of cups that had no handles. Mr. Tarlton acknowledged Phoebe's message, but made no great haste to leave. He explained to her that the smashed Goldfinch was taken care of. The police were not pressing charges against either party, and Cousin Henry Mottrell was paying for all the repairs. The Goldfinch would be ready to drive again tomorrow.

"Mr. Tarlton has gone to a lot of trouble to arrange everything for us. We should be very grateful," said Miranda with a meaningful look at Phoebe.

Before Phoebe could produce the proper "Thank you," Mr. Tarlton was talking again. It was no trouble at all. Cousin Henry wanted the accident kept quiet. He was glad to pay the damages and keep the insurance companies out of it.

"Now," said Mr. Tarlton, still showing no disposition to leave, "we must make a new date for our dinner together." He drew out a little notebook and a pencil. "When shall it be?"

A long discussion followed. Miranda felt they should only go out on Fridays and Saturdays. Mr. Tarlton said she was too conscientious altogether. Miranda was gentle, but firm. Mr. Tarlton sighed. He had to be in New York on business all the coming weekend, so, and he sighed again, they must put off the dinner to the following weekend. Would Friday do? He pointedly asked Phoebe first, and then Miranda.

Phoebe said, "Yes, thank you," and Miranda smiled

74

at her and then at Mr. Tarlton. She said it would do for her too.

Mr. Tarlton wrote the date in his notebook. Still he didn't leave. In New York, he went on, he could get another book on Japanese painting which he was sure would interest Miranda. Might he bring it to her Monday afternoon, when she got home from school? Miranda said he was too kind. They went on even longer, paying each other compliments. Phoebe rather hoped Miss Tarlton would rise up out of the stairwell and tell him to hurry up, but she never did.

When Mr. Tarlton finally left, Miranda hugged Phoebe and asked where she had been, and while they cooked supper Phoebe told her. Miranda listened, nodding and smiling, and saying how happy she was that Phoebe had friends, but she didn't ask questions about them the way Miss Tarlton had. She seemed to be in a sort of daze. After supper, Phoebe went over her homework lightly and hurried to bed, where she read herself to sleep with the Everest part of *Alone to Everest*.

[12]

PHOEBE GOT TO SCHOOL early next morning, bringing *Alone to Everest* along to give to Constance to take home to Harry, although she hadn't finished it. This gesture she hoped would remind Constance of her existence (which at the end of yesterday afternoon both she and Harry seemed to have forgotten) and of their shared enthusiasms. Thus reminded, and touched too by her generosity, Constance would, Phoebe hoped, invite her back to Dreamwold that afternoon. She posted herself in the corridor by the coatroom door, ready to meet Constance and present the book as soon as she arrived.

Almost at once Phoebe heard steps coming toward her, but it was not Constance who rounded the corner. It was Miss Dwight. Miss Dwight stopped short; Phoebe Smith was just the girl she wanted to see. She pounced on Phoebe and whisked her away. It was like being pounced on by Jehovah and whisked away in a thundercloud. For a minute everything went topsy-turvy. Then Phoebe came to in a chair in Miss Dwight's office. Miss Dwight perched on the edge of her desk and surveyed Phoebe with very bright, all-seeing eyes. What she wanted, she said, was a friendly chat. She had read Phoebe's essay on why she hated skiing and thought it clever. She smiled. Phoebe was too awe-struck to speak, or even to smile back. Miss Dwight went on to say that she herself had been awkward as a girl, and Phoebe had her sympathy. She saw no reason to torture children by forcing them to do things which frightened them. On the other hand, fresh air and exercise were necessary to develop healthy minds and bodies. If Phoebe would promise to walk four miles, three days a week, instead of going to ski class, she would be excused.

Miss Dwight smiled a gracious, all-knowing smile. Phoebe knew she should respond with expressions of gratitude and joy (which indeed she felt), but so awe-inspiring was Miss Dwight, who held both her own and Miranda's fate in the palm of her hand, that Phoebe could get out nothing better than a mumbled, "Thank you." Her sense of her own inadequacy overwhelmed her. Miss Dwight, in her all-knowingness, seemed to appreciate Phoebe's condition, for she gave up all pretense of a friendly chat and carried on alone.

Phoebe's schoolwork had not been at all what was required at Denby from girls of Phoebe's age and ability. Now, relieved of the ordeal of skiing, perhaps Phoebe would be more comfortable and happy and better able to do her lessons. It was always hard for new students to get used to the workload at Denby. They all had to study harder than they ever had before. Some whined, some sulked, some had temper tantrums, some even tried to run away, and here it seemed to Phoebe that Miss Dwight gave her an especially penetrating look. In the end, Miss Dwight went on, all but a few misfits found that, with patience and application, they could do the work after all. They learned to enjoy it. They took pride in it, and, by planning their time, they fitted in many other activities too. Miss Dwight would be very disappointed with Phoebe, if by the end of the year she hadn't risen to the challenge of Denby. Miss Dwight expected her to become a true Denby girl, a useful, happy, well-liked member of the community. With a smile and wave of her hand, she dismissed Phoebe.

Back in study hall, Phoebe gradually recovered her wits. Miss Dwight had not only put her on honor to walk four miles three times a week, but had demanded, in return for the skiing dispensation, that she do better in school — or else. Phoebe knew all too well that doing better meant understanding the math problems, learning exactly where the commas should go, and memorizing French irregular verbs. Miranda was right. Miss Dwight was a hard taskmaster, but, like Miranda, Phoebe didn't want to disappoint her. She opened her French grammar to the assigned lesson. "Negative Interrogative of Avoir," it said.

n'ai-je pas?
n'as-tu pas?
n'a-t-il pas?
n'a-t-elle pas?

How could she possibly get all that straight before French class? She couldn't, but she would try. She had been trying for some time when she became aware of something poking her foot from behind. She looked down. There on the floor lay a wad of paper with her name — Phoebe, not Feeble — written on it. Her heart leaped up. Though she had often passed notes for others, no one had ever before passed a note to her. She covered the note with her foot, glanced up to be sure the proctor wasn't watching, dropped her pencil, leaned down to pick it up, and picked up the note with it. She unfolded the note and spread it over the open pages of the grammar.

"WHERE HAVE YOU BEEN?" it said in block letters, and went on in longhand, "Harry wants to see you this afternoon. Can you cut skiing and walk to my house? I will cover for you at ski class attendance. Very Important. Answer yes or no. I'll explain everything at lunch." It was signed, "Con."

Happiness bubbled up inside Phoebe. She tore a sheet from her notebook and wrote,

"CAN DO. YOU DON'T NEED TO COVER FOR ME. SEE YOU AT LUNCH.
PHOEBE."

She folded the paper, wrote "Constance" on it, bent as if to scratch her ankle, laid the note on the floor, and with a quick backward scuff, sent it skidding under the desk of the girl behind her. A moment later, she heard the note being scuffed farther along on its way to Constance. No one could learn the Negative Interrogative of Avoir when all the delights and surprises of an afternoon at Dreamwold Castle were dancing in her head. Phoebe gave up trying.

"Where on earth were you all the first period?" demanded Constance. "I thought you must be absent."

Phoebe explained about her interview with Miss Dwight and the excuse from skiing. "I was so scared of her," she confided, "that I could barely talk."

Constance ignored the confidence. "That's great. You really do get the breaks," she said. "I guess it's about four miles to Dreamwold Castle and back. You could come whenever we needed you." She rustled through the pages of her notebook. "Here it is. It's a map Harry made so you can find the way to Dreamwold Castle — that's where we live. It's written on the gateposts. You can't miss it.

Phoebe studied the map. It was very clear. It even showed where she should turn off the main drive to go to the back door and wait for Harry to let her in. "I'll go right after school."

"Will you stop at the post office on your way and ask for an application for a post office box?" Constance asked very quickly, all in one breath.

79

"You want an application for a post office box?"

"Yes. Will you?" Constance leaned over toward Phoebe until her face was only a few inches away; her eyes seemed to bore into Phoebe's.

Phoebe shrank back. "What for?"

"Harry will explain. Will you?"

"I — I guess so. Who's it for?"

"It's for us, but if they ask you, say it's for your mother."

"Why?"

"I told you, Harry will explain. They probably won't ask anyway, so will you promise?"

"Well, O.K."

"Cross your heart and hope to die?"

"Cross my heart and hope to die."

"What a relief!" Constance fell back in her chair and drew a deep breath.

"You give the form they give you to Harry," she added.

"I've got *Alone to Everest* for him, too."

"That's good. If anyone sees you around the house or the grounds, and asks what you're doing, you tell them you're bringing a book to Harry. Anyone except Ida, I mean. You don't have to worry about her. Just smile and shake hands and rub your stomach and say 'yum yum' the way you did yesterday."

"Constance," asked Phoebe, "what happened yesterday, just before I left, when Ida told you those things that made you and Harry so scared?"

"Harry will explain that, too," replied Constance and turned her attention to her lunch.

[13]

PHOEBE TREMBLED as she asked the postal clerk for an application for a post office box, but he handed her the form without even looking at her. Light of heart now, she walked to the crossroad where Mr. Wade was directing traffic as usual. He waved to her.

"You look chipper," he called. "No worse for the accident, eh?"

"Thank you, I'm fine," replied Phoebe and waved back as she hurried across the street and on her way.

For once it was a fine day, and, on the far side of town where the houses stopped, the snow lay sparkling white on the fields. In the woodlots all the tree branches were frosted with snow. Old Mott's craggy side, glistening with ice, appeared and disappeared as the road wound along, up and down and around. The farther she walked, the more certain Phoebe felt that she and Ben had driven along this road when they had gone to climb Old Mott in October (pretending he was Everest), and she thought she recognized the side road which had led them into the woods. What an adventure it would be, she thought, to climb Old Mott with Constance and Harry! They would pretend it was another Himalayan peak and that they were famous climbers. She made up conversations they might have as they toiled upward. This passed the time so well that she reached the Dreamwold Castle gateposts before she had even begun to look for them. She climbed the drive, watching for the turnoff to the back door, and suddenly Harry himself popped out from behind a snowbank.

"Have you got the form?"

When she nodded and held it up, he did a short war dance. Then he gallantly relieved her of all her books and hustled her into the turnoff behind the snowbank.

"You're real cool," he said.

"I brought you *Alone to Everest* too," she said. "If anyone asks me what I'm doing here, I'll tell them I came to bring you the book."

"You're all right," exclaimed Harry.

Phoebe knew she should tell him that using the book to explain her being there was Constance's idea, not her own; but she wasn't harming Constance, and she would probably have thought of it herself, if Constance hadn't happened to think of it first. She looked modest and giggled.

"Come on," said Harry. "Ida's asleep, and nobody else is home. That's why I could get out to meet you, but Ida will wake up, and someone may come any time, and if I stay out very long it will be just like me to catch double pneumonia again and ruin everything." He set a stiff pace, and Phoebe followed him between the snowbanks to the back door.

"I'm going to do my coughing now," he said, "before I go in. Wait a minute." He doubled up in a spasm of coughs and wheezes which rose to a climax and subsided slowly. "O.K.," he said, blowing his nose, "we can go in now. If I'd waked Ida up with that, she'd know

I'd been out. Leave your stuff in the entry. Just bring the book and the form."

Ida was stretched out on the couch in her cozy corner. When Harry wakened her, she popped up, all starch and smiles and bursts of unintelligible sound. Phoebe shook her hand, smiled, nodded, patted her stomach, and said "yum yum," just as Constance had told her to, and Ida went into paroxysms of delight.

"Heaveaho," she cried as she helped Phoebe hoist Harry up in the dumbwaiter, and then she packed Phoebe in and heaveahoed her single-handedly up to the attic. Today the refreshments were doughnuts filled with jam. They were so delicious that Phoebe, hungry from her walk, ate one after the other.

"Go on," Harry encouraged her, "finish them. I can never eat all she sends up. I put a lot of stuff down the toilet, so as not to hurt her feelings." He cleared his throat. "I guess you want to know why we wanted you to get this application form."

Phoebe nodded. Her mouth was full.

"It's better for me to do the explaining," Harry went on, "because I'm logical. Con barges into the middle of everything and then gets all mixed up. I make things clear. First of all, we have an older brother."

"I know," said Phoebe. "His name is Tarlton, but you call him Tony."

"How do you know?"

"Miss Tarlton told me!"

"Who's she?"

Phoebe explained. Harry scowled.

"I remember her now," he said. "She used to come here when we were small. We called her Cousin Grace. Don't believe what she says about any of us, especially Tony. She's just an old gossip. Anyway, nobody knows about Tony except for Con and me. We're the only ones he tells what he thinks. We're the only ones he cares about. Tony despises ordinary people and what they dig. He'd rather be an honest robber than one of them. Tony'd like best to be an Indian and live in the woods, wandering from place to place, knowing all about the country and the animals that live in it, and eating only what he could grow himself, or catch, or kill with a bow and arrow, and being skillful and strong, and independent, and free."

Harry jumped up and began pacing back and forth. "Even when Tony was a little kid, he was always running off up on Old Mott. He'd cut school and skip meals and catch hell, but he couldn't stop. When he got older, he stayed out all night, and our mother went into tailspins and sent out search parties. They never found Tony. He had a Secret Place. He didn't want to worry our mother. He just wanted to lead his own life in the woods. He thought she'd get used to him after a while and stop worrying, and maybe she would have, if the Evil Eye hadn't kept butting in. The Evil Eye is what Tony calls our father. We call him that too, but not to his face the way Tony did. When the Evil Eye sounds off, it's scary, but Tony wasn't scared. He never lost his cool. He doesn't give a damn for the Evil Eye or anyone else, except Con and me, and Old Mott. It used to all belong to us, and this side still does." Harry stood by the window, looking out at Old Mott, apparently lost in contemplation.

He stood so long that Phoebe thought he had forgotten her. She cleared her throat. "Miss Tarlton says there is a vicious streak in the Mottrells."

Harry wheeled round. "She's got a nerve!" After a minute, he shrugged and sighed. "She may be right about the Evil Eye, but not about Tony. Tony just won't let anyone shove him around." Harry came back to the table and sat down. "I'm getting off the track, like Con. Tony sort of gets me going."

Harry collected his thoughts and went on. "Tony ran away from the boarding school the Evil Eye sent him to when he was sixteen. He stole a car to get away in and smashed it, and they caught him. He never could handle a car. The Evil Eye fixed things so Tony didn't get sent to jail, but he practically jailed him here. I was home, too, with asthma. After Tony's tutors left, I'd find a way to sneak in and talk to him to keep him company. When Con came home from school, we let her in. We brought Tony good things to eat from the kitchen. Ida knew we were snitching stuff for Tony, but she pretended she didn't. That was a great time for Con and me. We had Tony all to ourselves. We got to know him.

"That was when he told us about the Himalayas. He knew about all the big Himalayan peaks and who'd tried to climb them long before Everest was climbed and everybody started climbing new peaks and writing about them. Tony really dug George Mallory. Mallory was the only person in the world (except for Indians) that Tony wanted to be like. He made Con get him all the books about Mallory out of the library, and he read aloud to us from Mallory's letters and journals. Even though Con and I were so young, we got excited about climbing in the Himalayas just from listening to Tony read. We started planning then that when Tony was twenty-one and came into some money, we'd all three go to Nepal and live there and climb.

"Tony agreed to try boarding school again, and he stuck it out for almost two years, but he didn't do it for the Evil Eye. He did it to be worthy of Mallory because Mallory was so well-educated. When he was home for vacations, he took Con and me all over Old Mott to teach us how to live off the land and to harden us for climbing. We tracked animals and birds, and fished, and gathered mushrooms and ate them. Tony had learned all about mushrooms somewhere. He ate kinds that most people don't dare to, and he made us eat them and we didn't die. A lot of the time Tony is right, and the know-it-all grownups are wrong. We camped out all over the mountain, and Tony showed us his Secret Place that no one else knows about."

Harry suddenly banged the table with his fist. His voice rose. "I know I didn't get pneumonia from camping out with Tony, but our mother and the Evil Eye thought I did. They said he was killing me. Tony told them they were keeping me like a fox in a cage, and if I didn't get out and get strong, I'd waste away and die, and it would be all their fault. The Evil Eye blew his stack and threw Tony out. Tony wanted us to go away with him then, but I was sick and Con wouldn't leave me. Maybe if I'd gone off with Tony then, I'd be healthier now."

Harry paused and swallowed. "Right after that, our mother died. She had been sick off and on for so long that we hadn't noticed she was getting sicker. Tony came back for the funeral. He hadn't noticed either. If he had, he said, he wouldn't have said the things he did. He cried. Con and I are the only people who have seen Tony cry." Harry sat still for a while, lost again, apparently, in his memories. He shook himself.

"The Evil Eye tried to make Tony go back to school, but Tony wasn't taking any more orders from him. He joined the army to spite him. He hated the army even worse than school, and he ran away again and smashed another car, and they caught him and put him in the jug. No Mottrell had ever been in jail before, and the Evil Eye blew up. He went down to see Tony, and I guess they had the worst fight yet. Tony must have told the Evil Eye that he was taking Con and me away as soon as he got out.

"When the Evil Eye got back home, he called Con and me in and told us we were never to see or speak to or write to Tony again. Tony was a rotten apple, and if we associated with him, we'd go rotten too. I've never seen the Evil Eye more livid. He said that after all the trouble he'd had with Tony, and our mother dying and all, he couldn't take any chances with us. He said he couldn't keep Tony from getting the money he'd inherit from our mother — he could collect that from the lawyer as soon as he was twenty-one — but Tony wasn't getting a penny of Mottrell money, and he never wanted to set eyes on him again.

"We tried to stand up for Tony — Con even talked

back — and that gave the Evil Eye the idea that we were rotten apples already, and he'd better take special precautions to keep us from getting worse. He hired Gestapo to keep an eye on Con. My asthma was a good excuse for him to take me out of school and keep me home with tutors. I don't mind them — they don't spy — but Gestapo really gets in Con's hair. She made a plan to poison him with a mushroom Tony had shown us — get Ida to cook some for him, like a peace offering. She'd have done it too, if I hadn't stopped her. I told her she just had to be patient, Tony would come back, and he has. He's come twice, just to see us, and he camped in his Secret Place, and no one knew he was here except for Con and Ida and me."

Harry stood up and began to walk up and down again.

"It's dull between his visits, but we read all the books we can find about the Himalayas, and we made the model, and we save our allowance for travel money and to buy equipment. We want to find a hidden valley, like the sanctuary around the base of Nanda Devi, only easier to get to. We want to build a hut and grow some wheat and keep a yak for milk and yarn to make cloth, and we'll hunt the Abominable Snowman until we catch one and tame him and make friends with him."

"Oh," cried Phoebe, "that's what I want to do, too. When I'm in my Eagle's Nest, I imagine I'm living in a hut in Nepal with Tenzing and climbing mountains with him."

"You do?" Harry eyed her with interest. "What is this Eagle's Nest anyway? I never heard of it before."

Phoebe was embarrassed to have revealed so much of her secret life, but Harry's interest was flattering. She went on to explain all about the Eagle's Nest, how she had found it, and how she spent her afternoons there. Harry didn't laugh at her.

"That sounds great," he said. "I think Tony will dig you. He might even take you along with us."

In her mind's eye, Phoebe saw a little procession weaving its way up a flower-strewn slope toward the proud peaks: Constance, Harry, herself, a haughty yak, a woolly Snowman, and, up ahead, silhouetted against that blue, blue sky, Tony, leading the way.

All she could say was, "Gosh."

[14]

"I'LL ASK HIM when he comes," said Harry, "but first we've got to get down to business." He spread the application blank on the table. "What you have to do is very easy," he assured her. "You'll fill in the blanks here the way it says to, only, because you're a child you'll have to use your mother's driver's license for identification, so you'll have to pretend you are your mother instead of yourself. Where it says 'Signature of Applicant,' you sign her name. You may have to practice some before you get it to look right, but I'm sure you can do it."

"Isn't that forgery?"

"No, it's not, because we're paying for the box, and you're not affecting your mother's legal rights or obligations. I found that out from my tutor, the one who's studying law. You're doing your mother a favor."

"I don't think she wants — "

"You never can tell," put in Harry, "and anyway she won't know." He pointed to some small print at the top of the form. " 'The name, address, and telephone number of the boxholder contained on Form 1093 may not be disclosed except for law enforcement purposes, in response to a subpoena, or a court order'; and so on. No one can ever tell your mother she has that box. All you have to do is fill in the application the way I've told you, take it to the post office, along with two dollars that I'll give you, and give it all to the clerk. He'll tell you your box number and combination. You'd better bring your mother's license along too, just in case he wants to check the signature and the number. Be sure to learn the combination by heart."

"Why must I do all this?" asked Phoebe.

"Why?" Harry's voice rose and cracked. "Don't you see? So we can go on writing to Tony, and sending him money — it's not easy for him to get jobs because he has a bad army record — and so we'll know when he's coming again, so we can get his Secret Place ready for him, and so we'll know when he's planning to leave for Nepal, so we can get ready for that, too. You should know that you can't go on a Himalayan expedition without a lot of planning." Harry looked annoyed.

"You never told me all that," returned Phoebe reproachfully.

Harry fell back in his chair and thumped his head with his fist. "I'm sorry," he said. "You see, talking about

Tony sets me off. I forget to be logical. I'm as bad as Con. I'll explain it all. When Tony was here last October, he told us how to get a post office box, so we could write letters back and forth without the Evil Eye knowing it. We put Ida's name and Social Security number on the application blank. She didn't understand, but she didn't mind either. We wrote back and forth, and Con mailed our letters and collected Tony's, while Gestapo sat in the Fossil and waited for her to come out of the library or the drugstore or wherever she told him she was going. Everything went fine until Gestapo caught her coming out of the post office with a letter in her hand, when she had told him she was going to the drugstore for gum. She took off down the alley the wrong way, so he wouldn't try to follow her in the Fossil, but he did, and Zap! You know the rest."

Harry shook his head. "We burned the letter right off and wrote Tony not to write to us again until we told him to. Con managed to mail that one in the box near school. She pretended she had to go to the bathroom and snuck out and back, and no one caught her.

"I figured that Gestapo couldn't prove that the letter he saw Con carrying was from Tony, and running into you made him look such an awful fool, I thought maybe the Evil Eye would get mad at him and fire him for being incompetent. No such luck! Last night we had another showdown. The Evil Eye got Con and me in his study, one at a time, and he broke us. He can break anyone he wants to, except Tony. He made us admit about the post office box, and the letters, and about taking money from Barbara's purse to send to Tony. She'd been complaining to him about never having as much money in her purse as she thought. He was already suspicious. Now Con can't go anywhere without Gestapo standing right over her. I can't go anywhere anyway. As soon as Con's school stops, the Evil Eye is sending us to some place in Switzerland that's supposed to be healthy for people with asthma. There's an all-year-round school there, and we've got to go to it. It sounds awful, but if you'll help us, it won't happen.

"Con doesn't get out of school until June, and on May second Tony turns twenty-one and can get his money that our mother left him. As soon as he's got it, he can come for us, and before the Evil Eye can send us to Switzerland, we'll be off to Nepal! I've got it all planned." Harry's eyes sparkled. "I can't promise to take you along until Tony passes on you, but if you help us, I bet he'll want you along."

Phoebe was trembling. Here was real adventure as wild as any she had ever dreamed of.

"After you've got the box, all you have to do is stop at the post office once or twice a week to collect the letters from Tony and bring them to us. We'll give you the letters we write to him and you mail them. Con can't take any more chances. It's not a lot of trouble for you, and it means everything to Tony and Con and me — and you too, maybe."

"O.K.," said Phoebe. "I'll do it."

"Hooray!" Harry jumped up, grabbed Phoebe's hand, and pumped it. "I knew you were cool," he cried and immediately doubled up in a fit of coughing.

[15]

RIGHT AFTER SUPPER, Phoebe retired to her room, allegedly to do homework, actually to practice Miranda's signature. She had already snitched Miranda's license out of her purse on the hall table. The arrival of Mr. Tarlton, who had just popped up, so he said, was welcome for once. Miranda wouldn't be looking in on Phoebe as long as he was there.

Copying Miranda's signature wasn't the cinch Harry had made it out to be. The harder Phoebe tried to get the exact shapes and slants of the letters, the stiffer and clumsier her fingers got. She brought the electric heater out of the bathroom, plugged it in beside her, and warmed her hands at it. It was midnight before she was satisfied with her copies and dared to write Miranda's name on the blank itself. It looked very authentic. She returned the heater to the bathroom, hid the application and the license in her notebook, and went to bed. In the parlor, Miranda and Mr. Tarlton were still talking.

The next afternoon, although the signature still looked good and Constance had given her the two dollars and a pep talk, Phoebe approached the post office with fear in her heart. She laid her filled-out blank, Miranda's license, and the two dollars on the counter. The postal clerk looked them over.

"Mother send you?"

Phoebe nodded.

"Where's Mother? Why didn't she come herself?"

"Working," Phoebe managed to say.

The clerk turned away and disappeared in the back. Phoebe felt certain he had gone to call the postmaster and the police. She wanted to bolt, but a large woman behind her was blocking the way. The clerk came back with a card.

"That'll be two dollars," he said.

Phoebe shoved the money toward him. Her hands were shaking, but he didn't notice. He handed her the card.

"Tell Mother the combination is written here. Box rent is due quarterly." He looked over Phoebe to the lady behind. "May I help you?"

Phoebe scooped up the card and the license and ran. At the crossing she barely took time to wave to Mr. Wade. She raced full tilt out of town, then had to slow to a jog because the road was mostly uphill. The last stretch up the drive to Dreamwold Castle was torture — her lungs were near bursting and she had a pain in her side, but she kept straight on. Constance was waiting at the back door.

"Well?"

Phoebe held up the card. Constance jumped at her and hugged her so hard she knocked her down. It was several minutes before Phoebe could pick herself up, catch her breath, and be ready to greet Ida appropriately, climb into the dumbwaiter, and heaveaho up to Harry.

"Zowie," he shouted when he saw the card. "You're the coolest kid in town. Tony will dig you all right!" His smile shone over Phoebe, and she felt blessed.

Today, along with the coffee and whipped cream, Ida sent up a plate of cookies. Some were yellow, some were chocolate, and some were pink. They were shaped like clover leaves, rosettes, pinwheels, stars, and crescents. Some of the chocolate ones were rolled up to look like logs and sprinkled with green sugar, like moss. Some were miniature checkerboards with tiny alternating squares of pink and chocolate. Not even among the goodies Charlotte brought home from her weddings had Phoebe ever seen anything so delicate and beautiful. When she bit into them, they tasted like ambrosia, and she tried each shape and color while she told them how she had gotten the box.

Later, Harry gave Phoebe *Anapurna* to read while he and Constance wrote a letter to Tony. When that was finished, they all three discussed which mountain to make a model of next. Harry said Nanda Devi was out because the maps of it weren't detailed enough to be useful. He said he was impressed by all Phoebe knew about Nanga Parbat and the disasters that had happened there. He asked her to get all the books about it out of the library so he could reread them, and meanwhile he would let her have *Anapurna* over the weekend so she could finish it. The final decision would be between Anapurna and Nanga Parbat. Before she started home, Harry and Constance gave Phoebe instructions about the post office box. She was to check it two or three times a week, and she must never breathe a word about it to anyone. They said she could come to Dreamwold Castle to work on the model every schoolday afternoon, if Constance told her in school that it was O.K., but she shouldn't tell anyone where she was going. Phoebe said she thought she'd have to tell Miranda. They agreed that couldn't be helped, but Phoebe could tell other people that she was taking a long walk to make up for not taking skiing.

"And it's perfectly true in a way," exclaimed Constance. "Besides being so cool, you get all the breaks. I wish I was like you."

Phoebe smiled modestly. Then a scary thought came to her: What if she was already walking up the driveway to Dreamwold Castle and she met Gestapo, or, worse still, the Evil Eye — what should she say to them?

Constance and Harry consulted together. They thought she was unlikely to meet either one. The Evil Eye almost never came home before six in the evening, and neither did Barbara. When Gestapo wasn't driving, he was in the garage in back, fiddling with the Fossil or one of the other cars. If either one of them crept up on her before she could hide behind a snowbank, she'd just have to say she was bringing Constance or Harry a book they needed. She could say the same if she happened to run into Mrs. Jeffries or her daughter Janice anywhere around the house. They came up from Denby to clean and help out. The chances of meeting them were slim, since they only came mornings, unless there was a party, and they never came up to Harry's attic. Ida wouldn't trust them to clean up there. She did it herself. Ida, of course, was a friend and O.K.

Harry handed Phoebe the letter for Tony, all stamped and sealed and addressed to a town in New York State that Phoebe had never heard of. Constance lowered her in the dumbwaiter. Phoebe waved goodbye to Ida.

With the letter in her hand, *Anapurna* under her arm, and a wild happiness coursing through her, Phoebe hurried to the post office, then backtracked to the A&P, bought the groceries, and trudged home.

Although Miranda was off chaperoning for most of the weekend, Phoebe wasn't lonely. As soon as she had learned the combination to the post office box by heart and burned the card in the fireplace, she retired to her Eagle's Nest with the heater, *Anapurna,* and dreams of Himalayan adventures with her new friends. They vanquished the highest peaks, they caught and tamed the Abominable Snowman. At night, they sat around their fire of yak dung, eating chapaties, drinking tea laced with rancid butter, and discussing the exploits of the day. They were a band of heroes, all for one and one for all. No one was feeble or left out.

[16]

ON MONDAY MORNING, Constance told Phoebe that she could go to Dreamwold Castle that afternoon. She was to stop at the library, renew *Anapurna* and pay the fine (it was overdue), get out all the Nanga Parbat books she could find, and bring them to Harry. He would be waiting. Constance herself had to go to ski class.

As Phoebe came out of the library with her books, Mr. Wade waved to her, and, since there was hardly any traffic to direct just then, he escorted her across the street and lingered on the sidewalk to ask where she was going on this fine springlike afternoon. Phoebe hated to deceive her friend, but she had her orders. She told him she was setting out on a long walk instead of going to ski class, but said not a word about Dreamwold Castle or her new friends. Mr. Wade's eyes lighted when he heard about the long walk. He settled himself with his back against a big tree and proceeded to tell her about all the beautiful places there were to walk to in the woods and on the slopes of Old Mott.

Goose Pond was like a pearl in the forest. Now, in late winter, after all the freezes and thaws, you could walk in over the snow crust as easily as along a paved road. Here Mr. Wade admonished Phoebe to stay as much as possible off paved roads. They were death traps for walkers in winter. The old logging road up to Goose Pond branched off the main road less than half a mile out of town and was as safe as it was beautiful. If Phoebe walked up it a mile, she'd see the pond to her left, shining through the trees. It was spring-fed and never froze over completely. That was why the Canada Geese liked to stay there. If Phoebe walked in quietly, she'd see them.

But for a bracing climb and a fine winter view, he went on, you couldn't beat the Old Tarlton Trail up to the Old Tin Mine. The ox-track was still plain to follow through the woods and beyond, zigzagging between the boulders up the south slope of Old Mott. Mr. Wade paused, rubbed his chin, and studied Phoebe. She wanted to tell him that she had already been up the Old Tarlton Trail to the mine with Ben, as he ought to remember, but decided not to. He might take that as an excuse to ask about Ben or tell her about other walks, and Harry, she knew, was waiting.

"Thank you very much," she said. "I'll start right now."

"No," said Mr. Wade, and he laid a fatherly hand on her shoulder. "On second thought, I don't want you to climb up to the mine alone. It's supposed to be blocked up, but it isn't, except for the main shaft and the entrance. They could never block up all the little side shafts that went off into the mountain, and they've caved in, and if you don't know your way around pretty well up there, you can fall in. I wouldn't want any accidents happening to a nice kid like you." Mr. Wade smiled and patted Phoebe's shoulder, and Phoebe was about to say that then she'd go to Goose Pond and hurry off to Harry as fast as she could, when Mr. Wade added, "I felt different about that rapscallion Tony Mottrell in the old days."

Phoebe's impatience and boredom evaporated.

"Did you know him?"

"Know him!" returned Mr. Wade. "Everyone on the Force knew that one, from the time he was a nipper. That kid kept us busier than all the rest of the town rolled into one. Every time the little devil didn't feel like going home to dinner — which was pretty often, and in a way I don't blame him. It must be uncomfortable for a kid, living up there in that castle. Every time, as I was saying, the whole Force was called out to look for him. After the first few searches, we had a pretty good idea where he was. He was hiding out in one of those old mine shafts, either fast asleep or laughing at us. I told Mr. Mottrell as much and suggested that he wait until Tony had been missing a few days before he got upset and called us out. He said it was up to him to decide when the Force should be called out to look for his son. If we couldn't perform our duty to him as a taxpayer of Denby, he'd have us all fired. That was no idle threat," Mr. Wade went on. "In Denby, what Henry Mottrell says goes. After that, though, we didn't knock ourselves out to find young Tony, and if he had broken a leg, none of us on the Force would have shed a tear."

"Did you ever find his hide-out?" asked Phoebe. Her heart was beating fast.

"No, but I've got a good idea of where it is. I tell you what." Mr. Wade smiled. "Some nice spring day when the snow is pretty well gone off the mountain, I'll take an afternoon off, and we'll go up to the mine together and poke around a little. We might just find that hide-out of Tony's." Mr. Wade's smile got broader. "I'd like to leave a note there for him, saying I called."

Phoebe felt she must do her best to prevent this from happening. "If he's gone away, he'll never get your note. So what's the use of finding his hide-out anyway?"

Mr. Wade continued to smile. "You're a newcomer here," he said. "You don't understand. For all young Tony grew up to be a regular hell-raiser and ran away and smashed cars, and Lord knows what all, he always loved our mountain, just the way I do. If you're born and raised here, the mountain gets in your blood. Tony'll be back, and I hope he'll be reformed. He wasn't all bad."

Mr. Wade clapped his hand to his forehead. "What a dunderhead I am, boring you with old stories about

100

Tony Mottrell, who means nothing to you, when you should be on your way to Goose Pond, while the sun is still high. Here, let me keep your books for you until you come back. I'll just set them in the crotch of the tree here and keep an eye on them. You'll walk freer and faster without them." He held out his hands for the books.

Phoebe caught her breath. She was going to have to lie again, and fast. "Thank you very much, but I have to take them to a friend, a sick friend." She felt sick herself, having to lie this way to Mr. Wade. She couldn't look him in the face.

"You are a thoughtful little kid," he said. "I hope your friend doesn't live too far from the Goose Pond turnoff. There are other walks, of course — "

"She lives right on the way." Phoebe lied desperately on. She couldn't keep Harry waiting even longer while Mr. Wade described a whole bunch of new walks.

"That's good," said Mr. Wade. "Now remember the turnoff is just before you get to the top of the hill. You can't miss it." He gave directions for finding Goose Pond all over again. "As soon as the weather gets a little warmer, we'll take our hike up to the mine. Don't worry, I won't forget." He gave Phoebe a parting smile and a wave and walked back to his circle.

"Where on earth have you been?" demanded Harry. "I've been waiting over an hour." Phoebe explained, but Harry, rather than sympathizing, grumbled that Mr. Wade was an old windbag, and his walks were for old men like himself, and he didn't know anything about the woods, and if he ever tried to go up to the tin mine, he'd be trespassing on Mottrell land and liable to go to jail. "Who does he think he is, talking about Tony as if he knew him?" demanded Harry. His face flushed. He banged the table with his fist. "I thought I told you not to believe what people say about Tony!"

"I didn't say I believed it," began Phoebe.

"Then you shouldn't have listened to him," interrupted Harry.

"I couldn't help it."

Harry glared at her. She felt tears starting to her eyes again. She bowed her head and strove with all her might to keep from crying. If Harry sent her off in disgrace, she'd at least depart in dignified silence.

Distant shouts from Ida and the rattling of the dumbwaiter heralded the arrival of the food. Harry fetched it to the table. There followed, it seemed to Phoebe, a long and terrible silence. He cleared his throat.

"Look," he said. "I'm sorry. You can have all the jelly doughnuts, if you'll just stay and not be mad." He laid his hand on her shoulder. Phoebe lifted her head to look at him. He was smiling a timid, pleading smile. "Honest, I'm sorry. I mean it, and about the doughnuts, too."

"I tried to get away," Phoebe managed to keep her voice steady, "but Mr. Wade just kept on talking, and I couldn't help what he said about Tony, and I couldn't tell him to shut up. He's old, and he's a policeman, and my friend."

Harry patted her shoulder. "I can't expect you to drop your old friends because of me, but I rely on you so, I guess I forgot to be logical. You don't know how dull and lonely it is for me waiting up here for you to come. I imagine awful things have happened. Besides, it always sets me off to hear the things people say about Tony."

"It's O.K.," said Phoebe, and she smiled with relief.

Harry's smile widened. He gave her shoulder a final pat, and he poured the coffee. "Start eating," he said. "We've got a lot to decide."

They spent the rest of the afternoon in the friendliest way, poring over the maps and pictures of Anapurna and Nanga Parbat. When Harry decided that Nanga Parbat would make the more interesting model, Phoebe felt especially gratified. They would never even have considered Nanga Parbat if it hadn't been for her.

As she was getting ready to leave, Harry brought out a pile of letters for her to mail. They were not to Tony, but to various sporting-goods stores.

"I got the idea from the book you lent me about trying to climb Everest alone," said Harry. "That poor guy had to collect secondhand equipment in Africa of all places. We'll get catalogues of climbing gear, and we'll look them over while we're waiting for Tony, and when he comes we'll decide what to buy. That post office box of yours is really going to be useful."

[17]

No letters came from Tony during the next week, but the measurements and sketches for the model were finished, and, under Harry's direction, a skeleton of the mountain was built out of screening propped up with sticks. The next step was to spread a layer of plaster over the screening. After that, they would build up ridges, cliffs, and peaks out of more plaster, until the model looked like the picture of Nanga Parbat. This model would be larger than the one of Everest, and Harry expected it to be superior in every way.

At school on Friday, Constance approached Phoebe with a gleam in her eye.

"The Evil Eye and Barbara are going away tonight, and they won't be back until tomorrow around noon. Ida's going to cook a special dinner for us, and she says you can eat with us and stay overnight, too. Your mother'll let you, won't she?"

For a minute Phoebe was too overwhelmed to speak. "I suppose you'll have to ask her."

"I can't ask her because I can't interrupt her while she's working, but I can leave a note for her at home after school. It'll be O.K. with her."

Constance shook her head. "It must be wonderful to have a mother and be able to do whatever you want to, too. Come up right after you've left the note. I've got to ski, but you and Harry can start plastering, and

when I get home we'll play 'When the Cat's Away.'"
Constance's eyes gleamed brighter. She grinned her buccaneer's grin.

"We'll play what?"

"Wait and see. It's something we made up, the three
of us, when Tony was home."

Phoebe hurried home after school, packed a bag,
left a note for Miranda telling her where she was and
that she would be home for lunch the next day, and set
off for Dreamwold Castle.

As soon as she opened the kitchen door she sensed
festivity in the air. The kitchen, usually so dim, was
ablaze with light. As she stepped inside, a galaxy of
strange, delicious smells rushed to meet her and swirled
in tantalizing, ever-changing combinations under her
nose. At the stove Ida was beating something in a pot
and singing at the top of her lungs. Harry himself stood at the sink stirring something of his own. He
joined in the choruses of Ida's song by pounding out the
time with his spoon. The words of the song were unintelligible, but Ida's voice, blaring like a trumpet over
Harry's pounding, reminded Phoebe of nothing so much
as a cavalry charge. She couldn't resist bouncing up and
down, stamping her feet, and tossing her head. When
the song ended, Harry sank into a chair and coughed.
With his spoon he summoned Phoebe to take over his
stirring. Ida, not at all out of breath and beating strenu-
ously on, shouted a long greeting at Phoebe which ended
as usual with the cry of, "yum yum!"

"Yum yum!" Phoebe shouted back, and she banged
her stomach like a drum. Ida doubled up with laughter.

"I'm glad you can stay overnight," said Harry, with a nod at the suitcase. "If you think the plaster needs more flour, put it in. I can't seem to get the thickness right, and Ida's too busy with dinner to be much help."

Phoebe and Harry took turns stirring and adding to the plaster until it seemed right, but when they took it upstairs and tried to smooth it over the screening, it ran through. They took it back to the kitchen and added and stirred some more. Ida encouraged them with more songs and long speeches, which Phoebe guessed were advice. This time the plaster worked better, and they began to smooth it over the lower slopes. There were no refreshments, for Ida's special dinner had driven everything else out of her head, but Phoebe didn't miss them. Spreading plaster with Harry, who was in high good humor, was happiness enough, and the festive spirit of the kitchen had risen to the attic. The air tingled.

When the dumbwaiter shaft emitted a faraway hallo, followed by the usual creakings and rattlings, Harry's eyes lighted. He laid aside his work and stood up. A few moments later, Constance bounced out of the dumbwaiter and into the attic.

"When the cat's away!" she shouted.

"The mice will play!" replied Harry. He waved his arm. "Let's go!" He made for the door.

For an awful moment, Phoebe was afraid the two of them had forgotten her again and were going to dash off somewhere without her. However, Constance gave her a shove, Harry said, "Come on!" and they followed him to the backstairs. Halfway down they turned off through a door into a wide corridor and followed this

106

until they came to the top of what Phoebe recognized as the great double staircase she had seen from the foyer. They pelted down it and across the foyer. The carpet was so thick they seemed to bounce, and they made no sound. Harry opened a double door, snapped on a light inside and led them into a room more enormous and resplendent than even the foyer. Chandeliers hung sparkling from the ceiling, mirrors gleamed on the walls, festoons of pale satin shrouded the windows. Great soft sofas, chairs, and hassocks clustered here and there on a pale gold carpet. It was softer and deeper even than the carpet in the foyer, and it stretched on and on into the distance, where loomed an enormous object with black legs and a bulbous white body. At first Phoebe thought it was an elephant — in this room, anything was possible. It turned out to be a grand piano draped with a dust sheet.

"First we line up the hassocks," said Harry.

The hassocks were dragged to the far end of the room and arranged in three rows of three to form a square. The sofas — there were four of them — had to be moved and placed one along each side of the square, facing inward. Lifting and carrying the sofas was almost too much for them. They could only move one a few feet at a time before they had to set it down and rest. Harry had a coughing spell, but he wouldn't give up — luckily, for the girls could never have done the job without him. When the sofas were finally in place, they formed with the hassocks a padded platform about eight feet square, fenced around by the sofa backs. Harry pulled the dust sheet off the piano. He took off his shoes, climbed onto the piano bench and from there to the top of the piano. He rose on his toes, extended his arms to each side.

"When the cat's away!" he cried. Constance joined in. "The mice will play!" Harry took three steps across the piano, as if he were on a diving board, dove up and out, rolled up in a ball in midair, and landed, by a miracle, it seemed to Phoebe, neatly on the back of his neck in the middle of the hassocks. He bounced like an acrobat in a net, until he got his feet under him and bounced over the fence onto the floor. Then he made an acrobat's bow.

Constance was already on top of the piano, waiting her turn. "Watch this!" She rose on her toes. They both yelled, "When the cat's away!" Constance flew into the air, rolled up, landed, bounced up and down, and finally over the fence and onto the floor.

Over and over, they dove, rolled, landed, and bounced. Now they really had forgotten Phoebe. She watched them, half relieved at not being called upon to jump, half itching to give it a try. At length Harry stopped to cough and noticed her.

"Go on," he said, "jump. It's easy."

"What if I miss?"

"You won't," said Constance. "The first time, just jump feet first, like this." She demonstrated.

Phoebe climbed onto the piano, then decided to go back. Constance, however, had climbed right up behind her.

"Hurry up," she said. "We haven't got all night."

Phoebe knew her hour had struck. She walked to the edge of the piano.

"When the cat's away!" shouted Constance behind her.

Phoebe shut her eyes and jumped. She landed on her seat with her legs tangled up in the cushions so she hardly bounced at all, but she was quite unhurt, and the cheers and congratulations of Harry and Constance were so heartening that she determined to try again. She tried again and again. At each try she jumped more boldly, landed more gracefully, and bounced higher. Soon, she too was diving, rolling into a ball in midair, landing neatly, and bouncing as high as the others. "When the cat's away!" she shouted as loudly as they did.

Somewhere a telephone began to ring. They paid no attention. It rang a long time, but finally stopped. They jumped faster and more furiously. They bounced higher and higher. They tried comic variations and laughed until they collapsed in stitches on the carpet. Harry and Constance both heard a distant clock strike six, though Phoebe didn't. It was time to stop and push the furniture back. Ida mustn't suspect what they'd been doing. All together, they wrestled the sofas back to where they belonged. After that, Harry, who was wheezing, rested while the girls took care of the hassocks and put the sheet back on the piano. They put on their shoes and made their way, undetected, back to Harry's attic. When Ida called them to supper, they were washed and brushed, and Harry had got his breath back. They descended to the kitchen, one by one, in the dumbwaiter.

In her cozy corner, Ida had laid the table with a white cloth, and she herself had dressed up in what Phoebe guessed must be her native costume, a white blouse trimmed with lace, a black bodice, and a full black skirt with a band of bright embroidery around the hem. With her pink cheeks pinker and her blue eyes sparkling brighter than ever, Ida looked like a girl, and her gay skirt swung girlishly whenever she jumped up to fetch another dish from the stove. In all her life before, Phoebe had never tasted such dishes as Ida's. They started with creamy soup, went on to roast pork stuffed with prunes, and culminated in a glistening white tower of a cake which, when cut open, revealed three different layers, with two different fillings. Even the Old Mott Special, Phoebe reflected, would look pretty ordinary beside this creation of Ida's. While they all helped Ida wash up, Ida, Constance, and Harry sang songs in Finnish. Some were rousing and martial like the cavalry charge, some were gay, some peaceful, and one was like wind whispering through fir trees. Phoebe felt that she had heard it before, though she couldn't say when or where. This seemed to be a favorite, for they sang it over and over, until Phoebe could hum the tune along with them. After the dishes were washed and put away, Ida brought out a Parcheesi board and summoned them back to the table to play.

Phoebe had played Parcheesi before with Miranda and Charlotte and Ben in the old days, on evenings when there wasn't a movie worth seeing and Miranda was tired and wanted some mild amusement. There was nothing mild about Parcheesi as played by Ida, Constance, and

Harry. It was war. They contested each shake and each move, no holds barred, no quarter given, to the bitter end, and all in Finnish. Ida slammed her counters down as if she were swatting flies. When she counted to fourteen, she yelled out each incomprehensible sound more fiercely than the last. The final "fourteen" was a war whoop. When she suspected someone of cheating, she shouted and shook her fist so fiercely that Phoebe trembled. Constance and Harry, however, weren't a bit afraid of Ida and were every bit as ferocious; and they did cheat, too, whenever they thought they could get away with it. Ida's accusations rocked the kitchen. Constance and Harry howled back at her like a pair of indignant Finnish wolves, and then they'd all three pound the table so that the counters bounced, and no one was sure where they had been, and they all accused each other of cheating, so ferociously that Phoebe expected them to jump up and start hitting each other. Somehow, they managed to settle their differences short of a free-for-all, and at the end of the game, which Ida won, she brought out a bottle of a colorless liquor and four small glasses. Into each glass she poured a few drops. In the greatest good humor, she raised her glass to the children and shouted something. Harry and Constance, all smiles now, raised their glasses and shouted something back, then they all downed their liquor, raised a sort of cheer, and started another game.

The liquor just about burned Phoebe's throat out as it went down, but, once in her stomach, it produced a warm glow. After each game, no matter who won, Ida poured them each a few more drops from her bottle, and the warm glow in Phoebe's stomach gradually spread all through her, filling her with courage and even a degree of fierceness. She, too, whooped in triumph when she shook doubles and laughed diabolically when she sent someone home. As the evening wore on, she found herself counting to fourteen in Finnish. In Finnish also she shouted taunts which she believed meant, "Blockade! Ha, ha!" or "You're dead! Ha, ha!" or "Cheat, cheat! I saw you!"

Ida jumped up and pointed to the kitchen clock. It was past midnight. She wouldn't even let them go up to bed properly in the dumbwaiter. She shooed them up the backstairs and hustled Phoebe into a room next to Constance's. A moment after she had climbed into bed, Phoebe was asleep.

When she awoke the next morning and looked out her window, she saw the summit of Old Mott sparkling with sunshine and new snow. Constance came in. She was in high spirits. Harry hadn't had an attack of asthma, in spite of all the jumping he'd done and all the dust he'd raised. He believed that Ida's aquavit had warded it off. The new snow meant that Mrs. Jeffries and Janice couldn't get up the driveway until after it was plowed, and the snowplow was broken and wouldn't be fixed before eleven, so if Phoebe would hurry and get up, they could gobble down the pancakes Ida was making for their breakfast, and get in a few more hours at "When the Cat's Away" before anyone came to disturb them.

Ida's pancakes weren't ordinary pancakes. They were very thin, and you spread them with jam and rolled them up and ate them with your fingers. Phoebe could

112

have gone on eating them all morning, but Constance and Harry were impatient to start jumping. They hustled her off.

This morning, it seemed to Phoebe, she jumped more wildly and freely and with more daring variations even than Constance. She flipped, she rolled, she pretended to be the gym teacher doing a header on her skis, or Miss Tarlton falling downstairs. Constance and Harry laughed over her imitations and were inspired to try a double jump to show the Gestapo and the Evil Eye driving over a cliff in the Fossil. Constance very nearly missed the cushions, so they gave up imitations and instead tried to jump high enough to touch the chandelier. The noise of the plow backing and filling in the driveway warned them in the nick of time that Mrs. Jeffries and Janice would be right along and then the Evil Eye and Barbara. Practice had made them better at moving furniture, but the sofas were still slow work. Phoebe got out the kitchen door and down the driveway just in time. A car turned up it moments after she had turned onto the road back to Denby.

[18]

THE ROAD this morning wound through a fairyland of sunshine and fresh snow, but Phoebe didn't see it; she was still in her own fairyland with Harry, Constance, and Ida at Dreamwold Castle. When she found herself at Miss Tarlton's back door, she came to and remembered that she hadn't bought anything for Miranda's supper last night, or for their lunch today. Poor Miranda, who hadn't been feasting off Ida's goodies, or anything else, was waiting for her in there, cold, hungry, and alone. Phoebe's heart filled with pity. She decided then and there to invite Miranda out to lunch at the Mottrell Arms, and to pay with her own money. While they ate, she would tell Miranda all about her wonderful visit with Constance and Harry. This would surely cheer her up and compensate for the dismal, lonely evening and morning she must have spent. Phoebe bounded up the stairs.

"Hi," she called. "I'm back."

Miranda came out of the kitchen. She looked cross. "How could you?" she demanded.

"I'm sorry," said Phoebe. "I forgot to stop at the store, so I'm going to take you out for lunch instead, and I'm going to pay for it, too."

"I'm not talking about lunch," replied Miranda. "I'm talking about last night."

Phoebe hung her head. "I guess I forgot to buy groceries then too."

"Groceries!" exclaimed Miranda. "Who cares about them? I'm talking about our invitation. You forgot it. How could you?" Her eyes brimmed with reproach.

Phoebe stared at her. For the life of her she couldn't think what Miranda was talking about.

"He has been so kind to you," Miranda went on, "and he asked you especially and set the date to your convenience."

Phoebe's memory stirred faintly, and her heart sank.

"Do you mean Mr. Charles Tarlton?"

"Of course I do. He invited you to have dinner last night, and you accepted the invitation."

Phoebe sighed. "I didn't mean to be rude, Miranda. I'd never been asked out to spend the night before, and I just forgot about the dinner. Besides," she added with a surge of annoyance at Miranda for making so much of such an unimportant thing, "he asked me so long ago, I don't see how you could expect me to remember."

"He asked you a week ago yesterday," returned Miranda. "It's just ordinary politeness to ask people to dinner a week in advance. I'd have reminded you, but I never dreamed you could forget. And then," her voice rose in indignation, "when I found your note last night, I tried to telephone you at your friends' house to come right home while there was still time before Charles arrived. The phone rang and rang, but no one answered. I was very upset."

Phoebe said nothing.

"Charles told me not to worry. He said that house with the funny name where you were visiting — Dreamboat or something like that — is so big that no one can hear the telephone unless he happens to be in the same room with it. He said it was only natural for you to forget an invitation like his when friends your own age had invited you to spend the night. He stood right up for you, Phoebe, and wouldn't let me go in the car and fetch you home. He said it would be wrong to embarrass you in front of your friends."

Phoebe wished she could feel more grateful to Mr.

Charles Tarlton than she did. Miranda, however, made up for any lack of gratitude on Phoebe's part.

"He was so kind and considerate and understanding," she went on, smiling now for the first time. "He was so wonderful to me, I just had to forget my disappointment and cheer up. We had a lovely time, after all. We only wished," Miranda gave a little reproachful sniff, "that you had been with us to share it."

"I had a good time too," Phoebe hastened to say. "I'll tell you about it."

Miranda looked at her watch. "Not now. Charles is coming for lunch in half an hour. While you've got your coat on, run down and bring up some firewood. We'll eat cozily in front of the fire. I've been to the store — there wasn't a thing in the house — and I've baked a cake. It'll just be a simple lunch, but I hope it will be good, and you must remember to apologize to Charles for last night. Not that he expects it, but just tell him you didn't mean to be ungrateful or inconsiderate." She gave Phoebe a forgiving smile and hurried back to the kitchen.

Mr. Tarlton arrived punctually. Phoebe apologized, and Mr. Tarlton accepted the apology most graciously. They all sat down to lunch in front of the fire, which Phoebe had laid and lighted. Mr. Tarlton couldn't praise Miranda's cooking highly enough, but to Phoebe, remembering Ida's creations, everything tasted flat. She did not, of course, say so. That would have been rude. But, to hold her own in the conversation, she did describe some of the delicacies she had eaten at Dreamwold Castle. Miranda said they sounded awfully fattening. Mr. Tarlton said he had heard his cousin Henry Mottrell complain that every time he ate a dinner prepared by his old Finnish cook he came away five pounds heavier. She was a fine cook, but she had no understanding of calories, and since she neither spoke nor understood English Henry had no way of explaining them to her. Calories apart, she ruled the roost up at Dreamwold Castle and was a regular Tartar when crossed. Henry often complained that he wasn't master in his own house and wanted to fire her, but again, short of learning Finnish, he had no way to do it. Mr. Tarlton chuckled, and Miranda laughed as if he had told a really funny story. Phoebe felt certain that, for all his graciousness, Mr. Tarlton was just as mean inside as the Evil Eye.

A little later, he asked Miranda to go out with him to view the snow. After a fresh fall of snow in Japan, he always went out snow-viewing with Akiko. Today, Miranda must let him introduce her to this simple but sophisticated pleasure. He knew she would appreciate it. Phoebe could tell that Miranda was dying to go out with him, and since she herself could never be comfortable with him around, she offered to wash the dishes so they could start right off. In the kitchen, while they were clearing the table, Miranda hugged her and kissed her and told her how dear and thoughtful she was. Miranda had to tutor someone at four, but she'd be home by five, and they'd eat the remains of the lunch for supper, and Miranda would tell her all about snow-viewing. It did Phoebe's heart good to be able to make Miranda so happy so easily. As soon as the dishes were washed, she herself was able to grab the heater and climb up to her Eagle's Nest. Harry had all her books, but today she didn't need them. She had her visit to remember and enjoy all over again.

[19]

HARRY WAS SICK on Monday, Tuesday, and Wednesday (the good effect of the aquavit had worn off), but on Thursday he was well enough for Phoebe to visit, and on Friday she found the first letter from Tony in the post box. Harry and Constance grabbed it, read it, and spent the rest of the afternoon writing an answer, which they gave to Phoebe to mail on her way home. It was addressed not to Mr. Tony Mottrell, but to Mr. Anthony Moulton. When Phoebe asked about this, Harry answered rather shortly that if Tony chose to use different names, it was nobody's business but his own.

After that, a letter arrived about once a week. Answers were addressed to an assortment of names in an assortment of towns in New York State. Harry and Constance never let Phoebe read Tony's letters, or their replies. The afternoons they spent writing to Tony were a little dreary for Phoebe, who had to spread plaster on Nanga Parbat all by herself, with no one to talk to.

Otherwise, though, she was happier in the attic with Harry and Constance than she had ever been.

Through ice, snow, sleet, hail, and sometimes, as February wore into March, through sunshine and slush that held a promise of spring, Phoebe trekked to and from Dreamwold Castle. On afternoons when Harry was sick, or had doctor's appointments, Phoebe made a point of taking one of Mr. Wade's walks and stopping by, on her way back, to tell him about it. It salved her conscience to be able to tell him the truth sometimes, and, when she wasn't in a hurry to get to Dreamwold Castle, she didn't mind walking in the woods, or listening while he told her about more walks and climbs.

The sporting-goods catalogues had begun to arrive soon after Tony's letters, and they were a source of new pleasure. When Constance, Harry, and Phoebe got bored with plastering Nanga Parbat — there was a lot of it, and the work was slow — they turned to the catalogues and pored over the tents, parkas, boots, knapsacks, sleeping bags, the ropes and pitons and ice axes that were pictured in full color and described in detail. They checked back through their climbing books to find out what equipment each expedition had used and how satisfactory it had been. Based on what they learned, Harry made evaluation tables of each major piece of equipment they would need, to show Tony when he came. Sometimes Phoebe felt as if they were already in Kathmandu, with their gear stacked around them, and the Sherpas standing by, ready to take off. As she scampered home late, with the stars glittering above, and maybe a cold white moon hanging over Old Mott, she felt she was really scampering down the Khumbu Glacier to her base camp outside Namche Bazar.

Phoebe saw very little of Miranda these days. They communicated mostly by notes left on the hall table. When their paths crossed, they greeted each other affectionately and went their separate ways. Miranda was never cross. Phoebe, just back from an afternoon with Harry and Constance, had too much to think about to miss Miranda when she went out for the evening or to worry because it was nearly always Mr. Charles Tarlton with whom she went.

One morning toward the end of March, as Phoebe was settling herself at her desk for the first class of the day, Constance walked past her, dropped a book, and, as she stooped to pick it up, slipped a note into Phoebe's lap. The note said:

MEET ME BEHIND THE GYM AT LUNCH BREAK. DON'T EAT FIRST. HE'S HERE!

Phoebe caught her breath. "He" could only be Tony. Would he dig her? Would he take her with the others to Nepal? Surely he must, after all she had done. She couldn't bear to be left behind. But she couldn't count on it. Harry hadn't promised. What was Tony really like? She had no idea, and her fate lay in his hands. Teachers asked her questions and scolded her, and her classmates snickered because she was in such a fog and made such stupid mistakes. Time seemed to stand still. When the noon bell finally rang, she shot out of class and reached the meeting place ahead of Constance.

Here, in the lee of the gym, the sun beat down full force. The gym wall, when she leaned against it, felt warm, and the ground under her feet was soft and oozy. In the still, sunny air she sniffed spring. Her heart pounded. Not even her first lunch with Constance had been as exciting as this.

Constance rounded the corner. "Can you whistle?" she demanded.

"Whistle? Why?"

"Can you?"

"Of course I can."

"Well, that's something." Constance slumped against the wall beside Phoebe.

"Did he say he'd take me?" Phoebe held her breath.

"What do you mean 'take you'?"

"To Nepal, of course."

"Oh that. We didn't even talk about that."

Rebuffed, but hopeful still, Phoebe pressed her. "Did you talk about me?"

"Yes, and I've got to give you your orders, and Harry says I'd better get them straight." Constance paused and shook her head. Her forehead wrinkled in a puzzled frown. "We didn't expect him yet. It's only March. The snow's still on the mountain. He never wrote us he was coming early. We haven't got anything ready. Suddenly" — her eyes widened and she caught her breath — "there he was, standing at the foot of my bed. He said, 'Come on, Con. Wake up. We've got to have a pow-wow, and there isn't much time.' I followed him into Harry's room, and I was wide awake, but it all seems like a crazy dream." Constance blinked and shook herself.

"What did he say next?"

Constance didn't answer right away, and when she did she seemed to be talking to herself more than to Phoebe. "He never hugged us or said he was glad to see us, and he didn't ask how the model was coming on, though we'd written about it in all our letters. He didn't

121

even smile at us. He kept jumping up and looking out the window, and lighting cigarettes and putting them out, even though he knows smoke makes Harry's asthma worse. He kept saying he was in a hurry, that he had to have clean clothes and blankets, and some food, but we mustn't tell Ida he was here."

"Do you usually?"

"Of course. She keeps all the clothes and blankets and things that he can't leave in his Secret Place because of dampness. We don't even know where she hides them, and he can't get food without her." Constance sighed. "Harry finally made him see that, so he let us wake her up, and she got busy."

"Did he say anything about me?"

"He said he didn't want anything to do with strangers and trespassers, but Harry explained you were special, and without you he couldn't get cigarettes and the Boston *Globe* up at his Secret Place, unless he went downtown and bought them himself. He never used to smoke hardly at all, and he never read the newspaper, and he wouldn't explain why he wanted the things so badly." Constance shrugged her shoulders and spread out her hands in a gesture of helplessness. "I don't understand why, but you've got to bring him two packages of cigarettes, and the Boston *Globe* every afternoon after school. That's part of your orders."

"I don't think — "

"You've got to, and first I'll teach you what you've got to whistle. That's why I said to meet out here." Constance pursed her lips and produced a series of sour notes interspersed with blowing noises. "I'm so tired," she complained, "I can't even whistle. I couldn't sleep at all after he left, and Harry wouldn't talk to me, and Ida cried, and I felt like crying, too, because Tony acted so mean." Constance heaved a sigh and turned to her whistling again. Eventually she produced a tune which, after several repeats, Phoebe recognized as one they had sung at Ida's party — the one that sounded like the wind in fir trees. Once she had caught on, Phoebe learned the tune quickly, which was a good thing, because the bell for afternoon study rang. Constance pulled a folded paper and a ten-dollar bill out of her pocket and thrust them at Phoebe.

"Harry's made a map to show where you take the cigarettes and the paper to. When you get to the place that's marked 'X' on the map, stop and whistle the first two lines of the song. Tony'll whistle back the next two. Then you wait until he comes. I hope I got it all straight."

"How do I buy the cigarettes? It's illegal for me because I'm too young."

"You'll have to figure that out for yourself. Harry didn't say."

"What if I get lost?"

"You won't. You just follow the Old Tarlton Trail. Harry's put it all on the map. Come on!"

"Will you and Harry be there too?"

"Of course. Hurry up. They'll keep us after if we're late."

[20]

As soon as she was at her desk in the study hall, Phoebe opened the map and looked it over. It was detailed and clear. Also, from her climb with Ben in the autumn, she was quite sure she remembered the turnoff from the main road to the side road, and how that narrowed down to a cart track and then to the Old Tarlton Trail. She was to whistle from the terrace in front of the Old Mine entrance. Harry had not only marked it with an X but also drawn a sketch of it. It was the same terrace Mr. Wade had described to her.

Next she considered how to get the cigarettes. She would never dare to ask for them at the A&P or the drugstore where everyone knew her, but there was a cigarette machine at the back of the variety store where they sold the papers, and she figured she could get cigarettes from it unnoticed, while the clerk was up front. If he caught her, she could always say they were for her mother, and she wrote a note to that effect in a good imitation of Miranda's hand and signed it with Miranda's name, just in case. Practiced deceiver that she had become, she even planned how she would avoid Mr. Wade by taking the alley behind the post office, crossing the Paxton Road where he wouldn't see her, cutting along the service alley behind the stores to the loading door of the A&P, through the store, out the front door, and, when Mr. Wade's back was turned, making a dash for the variety store. It was at the far end of the business district. From there on, she would be safe. She just couldn't risk being seen by Mr. Wade. It would be just like him, now that spring was coming, to decide to take her on that excursion up to the Old Mine, and Phoebe was dead sure that Tony would never take her to Nepal if he caught her snooping around his Secret Place with a policeman.

As soon as school was out, she executed her plan neatly and, with the Boston *Globe* under her arm and the cigarettes in her coat pocket, got an early start up the Old Tarlton Trail. At first the trail was muddy, but, where the woods got denser, snow still covered the ground. This snow didn't provide the firm walking surface Mr. Wade had promised earlier and was very deep besides. Every few steps the crust gave way, and Phoebe sank to her knees, sometimes to her thighs, so suddenly that, often as not, she lost her balance and fell on her face. She hadn't taken the time to change to ski pants or overshoes. After five minutes of thrashing about in the snow she was soaked through, and so was the newspaper, though she tried to hold it up when she fell. When she finally worked her way out of the woods and the snow to the steeper, more exposed part of the trail, she found that it had been appropriated by a rushing brook. She had either to wade against the current, which sloshed up over her ankles, or find detours. These got her into such trouble with ice, mud, rolling stones, and slippery ledges that she was grateful to be able to scramble back to the trail in one piece and wade on.

She made no faster progress than she had through

the snow. The exertion of struggling on kept her from feeling cold, but she was wet, muddy, and nearly exhausted when she finally clambered up onto the terrace in front of the Old Tin Mine, where the trail stopped. She was far too out of breath to whistle. She rested a minute and looked back over the difficult slope she had climbed. Remembering what Mr. Wade had said about the view, she took another minute to look out at that. Far down, on the lower slopes, she recognized the turrets and gables of Dreamwold Castle and realized that those same turrets and gables were what she had looked down on on her climb with Ben, and named Thyangboche Lamasery. Just a little higher up, it must have been, that she and Ben had heard the tune whistled back and forth and had pretended that they were hearing two Abominable Snowmen calling to each other, only Ben had said he didn't believe Abominable Snowmen could whistle tunes.

In a flash Phoebe knew why Ida's song that was like the wind in the fir trees had sounded familiar; it was the same tune she and Ben had heard, the tune she was about to whistle. She smiled. Wouldn't they all be surprised when she told them how she had heard them whistling to each other over six months ago, before she even knew them!

Would they remember the day? Had they had any inkling then that trespassers were about? If they had . . . Phoebe caught her breath. Trespassers were what Tony hated most. Just last night, Tony had said he didn't want any strangers or trespassers around. If he learned that she had once been a trespasser herself, wouldn't it ruin her chances with him just as surely as if he caught her snooping around with Mr. Wade? Phoebe determined never to let on that she had been here before with Ben. She felt all weak and shivery to think how with a few careless words she might have ruined the great chance of her life. The sun had gone under a cloud, a harsh wind had sprung up and was flapping her wet skirt against her wet legs. It was high time for her to whistle. Tony must be getting sick of waiting and was probably feeling meaner every minute. Constance had said he was mean. The harsh wind brushed over Phoebe again. Maybe she'd better not meet Tony, not today anyway. She would put the paper and cigarettes down where he'd see them, whistle, and run before he could get to her. But it was too late; Tony was standing beside her.

He was tall and broad-shouldered and dressed all in black. "I've been waiting for you to whistle," he said. "I thought maybe you'd forgotten the tune." He took the paper from her. "Got the cigarettes?"

Phoebe fumbled for them in her pocket. Her hands were shaking so, it seemed an age before she got them and the change out. Tony took the cigarettes.

"Never mind the change," he said.

Phoebe watched him tear at the cigarette wrappings. His hands were shaking too, and Phoebe suspected it was because he was angry at her for being late and getting everything so wet. Even the cigarette wrappings were wet.

"I'm sorry," she faltered. "I kept falling down in the snow."

Tony struck a match on the seat of his pants, lit a cigarette, and took several puffs before he said, "You made it anyway. That's more than the kids did. I had to pull them out of a drift." He inhaled, blew out the smoke, and stared off over Phoebe's head.

Phoebe stole a quick glance at him. He was like a tough guy in the movies, and like Constance too. His hair was blond like hers, only greased down, and he stood like her, with his chin up, as if he were accosting someone. He had Constance's regular features too, only bolder and stronger, but he hadn't her fresh color, and there was something drawn, almost twisted, about his mouth and jaw that reminded Phoebe of Harry, especially when he was getting over an attack. There was a stubble of reddish beard on Tony's chin, and his chinos and leather jacket were the worse for dirt and wear. He tapped the ash off his cigarette and looked down at Phoebe as if he had forgotten she was there and now suddenly remembered her again. His eyes were as blue as the twins', but they were lusterless and without expression. As she looked up at him, it seemed to Phoebe as if he had turned his eyes off, intentionally, to keep her from knowing him. She began to shiver worse than ever.

"Ever been here before?" asked Tony.

Phoebe shook her head.

"See anyone on the way up?"

"No."

"Anyone see you start off or know where you were going?"

"No."

After a pause during which he puffed on his cigarette, he said, "I guess you're O.K. You can dry off by the fire. Come on."

He jumped off the side of the terrace, waited for Phoebe to scramble after — she would never have dared such a jump, even on level ground — skirted the slope for a short distance, then turned straight up and wove a way among clumps of scrub and between boulders until he stopped beside a thicket of stunted fir trees. He waited for Phoebe to catch up, then pointed into the thicket. Phoebe saw a hole with the end of a ladder sticking out.

"Go on down," said Tony. "The kids are there. I'll be along in a minute."

[21]

PHOEBE WRIGGLED her way through the fir branches and started down the ladder. The last she saw of Tony, he had thrown away his cigarette and was opening the *Globe.* She climbed down into an increasingly dank and chilly twilight which smelled of smoke and mold. When her feet touched bottom, she made out by the light of some candles set in niches in the walls that she was in a large cavern cut out of the rock. In the center of it a stove made out of an oil drum split lengthwise and covered with a sheet of iron was spitting and crackling and glowing red. It provided an oasis of light and warmth in the chilly gloom. Harry sat at the open, glowing end. His feet were propped up against the stove top, and he was bent over, wheezing for breath. To one side, at a table, Constance was unpacking a hamper of clothes and food.

Harry straightened up. "Hang your coat on the line," he said, pointing to a rope strung across a corner of the cavern. "Stick your shoes under the stove. You can sit here by me and warm your feet." He moved over to make room and went on wheezing.

"I'm glad you got here," said Constance. "Now that Tony's got his old newspaper and cigarettes maybe he won't be so crabby."

"Lay off him," said Harry between wheezes.

"He's the one should lay off," retorted Constance. "He can't expect us to carry all this stuff through drifts up to our waists and not get pooped. Especially you, when they haven't let you out all winter. What does he think we are?"

Harry smothered a cough and shouted, "I told you to lay off." Constance snorted.

While Phoebe hung her coat and laid out her shoes and socks under the stove, drips kept landing on her head and shoulders. More drips landing on the stove made it hiss. Phoebe looked about. The cavern was roundish. Two passages led off from opposite sides, and transversely two more passages had been widened and blocked to form two recesses. In one Phoebe made out a bed, in the other, shelves. Apparently Tony had scooped out and enlarged the intersection of two of the mine's old tunnels. The floor was packed dirt with some planks laid across it. The walls and ceiling glistened with moisture, the drips fell gently and persistently, and beyond the oasis of the stove, it was mortally cold. Phoebe found a chair, drew it up beside Harry's, sat down, and stuck her feet up on the edge of the stove. Almost at once she began to feel warm. Hot air surged out over her as it had from the registers in her pretend caves in Putnam Park. Those olden days, she reflected, had been safe and happy, but now she was in a real cave, with real companions, and Tony, for all he'd been so gruff, had guessed she was O.K. She had carried out her orders, and she hadn't actually lied about being there before. She had managed well. She wiggled her toes in the warmth, spread her skirt to dry better, and reveled in the triumph of having actually been admitted to Tony's Secret Place. Constance plumped a coffee pot down on top of the stove.

"Anyone besides me want some cake now?" she asked. "I'm too starved to wait for coffee, and Ida's sent up so much food he can't possibly gripe if we eat a little without asking his royal permission first." She tossed her head.

Harry refused cake with an angry grunt. Phoebe was suddenly so starved she could hardly wait until Constance brought her a slice. Constance settled herself with another slice in a chair beside Phoebe and stuck her feet up against the stove too. Harry began to breathe more easily. Constance finished her cake, sighed, leaned back, and shut her eyes. Phoebe did the same, and a wave of drowsiness overcame her. She woke up with a start. Tony was standing over her.

"You sleeping beauties have got to shove off," he said. "It's going to rain."

"We just got here. We haven't had coffee." Constance sat up and glared at Tony.

"Tough," he said. "You should have got here earlier."

"We came as soon as we could, and it wasn't our fault the drifts were so deep. It was yours for coming so early, and you never let us know either. You've hardly said a decent word to us since you got here. You haven't told us anything." Constance shouted back.

"I'm telling you now. You've got to scram."

"What about Nepal?" demanded Constance.

"What?"

"Nepal? When are we starting?"

Tony stood still for a minute, then he pulled out the packet of cigarettes. "We'll talk about it later," he said. "Don't bug me. You've got to scram."

"I'm not bugging you. It's the first time I've even mentioned it," Constance jumped to her feet, "and you know you shouldn't smoke when Harry's around."

"Who says?"

"I do. Because of his asthma," retorted Constance. "You know that. What's the matter with you, anyway?"

"Nothing. I just forgot."

He was returning the cigarettes to his pocket, when, with a resounding pop and a loud swish, the coffee pot boiled over. Tony sprang back, reached inside his jacket and pulled out a revolver. He crouched against the wall. The whites of his eyes and the barrel of the revolver glistened as he shifted his aim back and forth from the ladder to one and then the other tunnel. Constance cried out and grabbed the coffee pot off the stove. She gave a louder cry, dropped the pot, and jumped up and down shaking her burned hand. The pot clanked down onto the floor. Spilled coffee and grounds steamed and sizzled all over the top of the stove. Tony put away his revolver, reached for his cigarettes, hesitated, put them back in his pocket, pulled out a handkerchief, and wiped his forehead. With the toe of his boot, he poked at the coffee pot. The spout hung loose, and the lid, broken off at the hinge, rolled away across the floor.

"That's it," said Tony. "Scram!"

Constance burst into tears.

"Keep your shirt on, can't you!" hissed Harry, and he grabbed Constance by the shoulder and shook her. Constance wrenched herself free and cried louder.

Suddenly Tony had pushed Harry aside and was holding Constance in his arms, patting her back, stroking her hair, murmuring to her. Constance threw her arms around his neck and buried her face in his shoulder. Tony held her and patted her and murmured to her until gradually she let him wipe her eyes with his handkerchief. Finally she took the handkerchief herself and blew her nose into it.

"I'm sorry, kids," said Tony. "You don't understand. I'm tired. I need to rest. Just wait. Maybe everything will be all right."

Constance nodded and managed a faint smile. Tony took back the handkerchief and wiped his face again.

"You can all come back tomorrow," said Tony. "Ask Ida to send up some more food, and — wait a minute." He disappeared into the alcove where the bed was and came out with a bulging paper bag. "Here's my laundry.

She can do it for me." He handed the bag to Harry. "Remember to be careful, and for God's sake don't get pneumonia." Harry bowed his head. "I'm sorry," said Tony after a minute, "I know you can't help it." He laid his hand on Harry's shoulder. "I'll go with you to the edge of the woods and help you through the drifts. I forgot how deep they get."

When they all had their shoes back on and were ready to go, Tony pulled a ten-dollar bill out of his pocket and handed it to Phoebe. "Buy me a new coffee pot and bring it up tomorrow, along with the paper and the cigarettes."

"I've got a lot of money left," said Phoebe, fishing it out of her pocket. "I don't need any more, unless you want a really fancy coffee pot."

"I want a good, plain coffee pot for boiling coffee," said Tony, but he made Phoebe keep both her change and the bill. "You might need it," he said.

He escorted them all out by one of the tunnels, which surfaced higher up the slope. "You got up by yourself," he said to Phoebe with a faint smile, "so I guess you can get down. I'll see you tomorrow. Keep your mouth shut, and don't forget to whistle."

The rain started when Phoebe was halfway down the trail, but it was just a drizzle, and her clothes were still wet anyway. On a detour through the A&P, she bought a steak, a package of frozen peas, and an apple pie, carefully keeping Miranda's grocery money separate from Tony's. In the apartment, on the hall table, lay Miranda's note, with the usual border of circles and crosses for hugs and kisses, and the usual message to the effect that she was having dinner with Charles and hoped her dear Phoebe had bought herself something good to eat for supper. Phoebe was relieved not to have to lie to Miranda about how she had gotten so muddy. She could hardly stay awake long enough to eat her pie. There was no question of doing homework. She washed the dishes and went straight to bed.

[22]

THE NEXT DAY was more springlike than ever. Phoebe hurried home after school to change to dungarees, a light jacket, and snow boots before setting off on the afternoon's business. She bought the coffee pot at the hardware store, and the newspaper and cigarettes at the variety store, without being questioned by anyone or being seen by Mr. Wade. Today she made faster work of the drifts and the trail-turned-stream. Just the same, the climb was hard work, and she was hot and panting when she scrambled up onto the terrace. Tony answered her whistle and, muttering that they showed up there like sitting ducks, hurried her away, not to the Secret Place, but higher up the mountain to what he called the Nook. It was a hollow he had made by clearing out a collapsed mine tunnel and piling the debris around it in a sort of wall. The wall, overgrown with brush and juniper, hid the hollow so completely that Phoebe would have fallen in if Tony hadn't been just ahead of her.

Inside the Nook, under the sun and out of the wind,

it was warm as summer. Harry and Constance were there already. Tony went off a little way by himself, lit a cigarette, and opened the paper. Harry was obviously exhausted, but Constance was in high spirits. Because of the unseasonably warm weather, she told Phoebe, ski classes were canceled for the rest of the season, and she had gotten permission to take walks instead of working out in the gym. She could come to see Tony every afternoon, too; the Hostile Powers were hardly ever home now. Ida was in charge, and Ida loved Tony. She had sent up cookies and jelly doughnuts. Tony was going to let them take the food to Big Slab and build a fire there and make coffee. She took the coffee pot from Phoebe, admired it, and stuffed it into a knapsack she had beside her. Tony snuffed out his cigarette and put away the paper under a stone.

"O.K.," he said. "Give me the knapsack. Harry, you follow me. If you feel like pooping out, say so, and we'll stop. You girls follow Harry. We're taking Fox Path."

Tony led them very quickly and precipitately down the mountainside to the edge of the woods. Phoebe slipped twice and skinned her hands and elbows, but she kept quiet about it. She had seen both Harry and Constance ahead of her fall and get up rubbing various parts of themselves, but not saying anything.

At the wood's edge, Tony turned and traversed the slope, keeping just under the trees, but avoiding the worst of the drifts. The path, a faint one at best, was now strewn with boulders, which got bigger and bigger and more numerous until the whole mountainside was covered with great slabs of rock, all tumbled together.

136

It was an ocean of rock, with a tree or a few bushes sticking up here and there like masts of storm-tossed ships among the waves. Tony went on from boulder to boulder as swiftly and surely as if he had been following a flat trail. He never hesitated or backtracked. What Phoebe thought of as his Band followed as best it could. Phoebe felt clumsy compared to Constance, who leaped along just in front of her and seemed to know when to use her hands and where to put her feet. Harry was wheezing and panting. Phoebe wished he would call a halt, but he struggled on, and Phoebe bent all her attention on her feet and the ground just ahead. Suddenly she ran smack into Constance, who was standing stock still, as were Harry and Tony, too. They were staring up at the biggest slab yet, and Phoebe just caught sight of a small reddish animal as it jumped off the big slab and vanished with its long, bushy tail floating behind.

"That's him," cried Tony. "I even saw the nick in his ear."

"I saw his tracks," gasped Harry. "I saw them once in the snow and once in the mud before we got to the rocks, but I didn't think they were fresh. Did you think they were fresh, Tony?"

"I wasn't sure. It's been so long since I've seen fox tracks. He was taking a sun bath and he must have dropped off to sleep. We didn't track him, Harry. We were just lucky."

"He looked right at me," said Constance, "and grinned."

"Foxes don't grin," said Harry.

"He did."

"Don't argue," said Tony. "I'm going to look around a little. There may be a vixen with cubs not far away."

"Get me a cub for a pet," said Constance.

Tony smiled. "That's easier said than done. The Old Lady isn't likely to doze off in the sun, not if she has cubs." He tossed his box of matches to Harry and disappeared.

The moment Harry caught the matches, he began to take charge. He chose a spot for a fire up against Big Slab and sent Constance out first for dry grass and spruce twigs, then for small dry sticks. With the sticks he made a little wigwam over his pile of tinder. When, on the second or third try, he got the tinder and sticks lighted, he ordered more and bigger sticks. Constance collected them and handed them to him as he needed them. When the fire threatened to die, Constance knelt down and blew on it until it came up again. When the fire was finally blazing, Harry got out the coffee pot and handed it to Constance who, without a word, set off with it into the woods. All this time, Phoebe had followed around after Constance trying to be helpful and keep out of the way. Obviously she was not needed. Now, feeling more awkward and useless than ever, she followed Constance through the woods for what seemed a long way and finally down a steep ravine to a brook. Constance set about rinsing the coffee pot and filling it.

"Do you know where we are?" asked Phoebe.

"We're at Lower Slab Brook," replied Constance.

As Phoebe followed Constance back up the ravine, she wondered if she could ever become a true member of Tony's Band. The others seemed to understand him and each other by telepathy. They could build fires and track animals. To them the wilderness was as familiar as Putnam Park used to be to Phoebe. For them the paths, the rocks, the brooks were like old friends with nicknames. Phoebe slipped and stumbled as she hurried to keep up with Constance, who bore the coffee pot up the slope and through the trees without spilling a drop.

When the coffee was cooking, Harry sat back against Big Slab and had a good cough.

"Do you want to climb around Little Slabland now?" asked Constance.

Harry shook his head. "I'm too pooped, and anyway, I want to watch the coffee, so it doesn't boil over. That might set him off again."

"I wonder why he acts so funny," said Constance.

"Don't," replied Harry. "You'll tire your brain."

Constance scowled at him, then shrugged, and turned to Phoebe. "I'm going to Little Slabland. You can come if you want to."

On the other side of Big Slab was a waste of smaller slabs all jumbled together. Constance jumped from one to another and pointed out to Phoebe the caves and burrows between the slabs. Some were just big enough for one person to crouch in, some were like small rooms. Constance jumped down into one and showed Phoebe how you could crawl from it into another. Phoebe scrambled after Constance through the maze of tunnels and burrows which joined cave to cave like the streets of a secret underground city. What a wonderful place to make up stories about or to play cops and robbers in.

Phoebe could have gone on exploring for hours, but Constance stopped in a cave just big enough for the two of them and looked up at the patch of sky that showed beyond the overhang of slab.

"We always hid in this one when we played Indians. We thought he couldn't find us, but he always could." She smiled a gentle, faraway smile — quite different from the buccaneering one Phoebe had grown used to. "Sometimes our mother sat on a slab and watched us play. He was so different then."

"Who do you mean?"

"Tony, of course, but you wouldn't know about it. It was a long time ago."

Once again, and more than ever, Phoebe felt what an outsider she was, a trespasser even, among her new friends. For a minute she wanted to run home, but the apartment wasn't really home. Miranda wouldn't be there anyway. Home and all her own happy childhood memories were far away with Charlotte in Putnam Park.

Phoebe drew a deep breath and tossed her head in imitation of the more familiar, buccaneering Constance. She felt her eyes flash and her determination harden. No matter what, she must become a full-fledged member of Tony's Band. For her there was nothing else.

The signal whistle sounded from the other side of Big Slab. Constance climbed out of the cave.

"Come on," she said. "Let's hope he's still in a good mood."

Tony was in a good mood. He told the girls to help themselves. He and Harry had already started. He thought he had found one of the vixen's burrows — of course she had more than one — and he had found the remains of a rabbit, most of it eaten, and there were fox tracks around it. He explained that, while the vixen was still nursing her cubs, she started them on half-digested meat that she ate and then threw up for them. Later, she brought them dead game to chew, then live game, so they'd learn how to kill. In the autumn — cubs were born in February — she'd teach them to hunt. Right now, Tony thought, she'd still be feeding the cubs on pre-digested meat inside the den, but on warm days she'd bring them out in the sun to play. He thought he'd found one of her play yards among the slabs in Upper Slabland. She'd chosen it for safety. She'd have a good view from it in all directions, and she'd be on constant alert; but if they were all patient and careful and lucky, they might be able to creep up on her some afternoon and get a good look. There was nothing prettier than a vixen with her litter of cubs. He finished his doughnut and grinned. The twisted, drawn look was gone from his jaw. His eyes shone as bright and blue and open as the spring sky.

"I'd rather have a fox for a pet than a yak," said Constance. "Will there be foxes in Nepal, too?"

Tony's head gave a funny jerk. His face went stiff. His eyes turned to stone.

"Don't ask stupid questions," growled Harry.

"I don't see why it's a stupid question."

"That's because you're stupid."

"I am not."

"Shut up."

"Both of you shut up!" Tony jumped to his feet.

"If you can't keep from fighting, if you can't keep discipline, I'll never take either of you anywhere." He gave them a cold, hard stare. They dropped their heads. "Clean up the campsite," said Tony. "You've got to get home."

He walked a little distance away and smoked while Harry and Constance doused the fire and packed the knapsack. Again, they both knew exactly what to do and Phoebe stood by feeling useless. Tony shouldered the knapsack and led the Band downhill until they had left the slabs behind and were in the deep woods. He waited while they floundered through the drifts, but he never spoke to them, or even smiled. Suddenly, to Phoebe's astonishment, they came to the edge of the woods just above Dreamwold Castle.

"Scram," said Tony, with a jerk of his head.

Harry hesitated. "What about tomorrow?"

"If it's safe and you can keep discipline, O.K., usual time."

Phoebe was about to follow Harry and Constance down the slope, but Tony told her to follow him and took her over to the Old Tarlton Trail where she was less likely to be seen. There he left her.

[23]

TONY AND THE BAND spent the next several afternoons in Slabland either stalking or lying in wait for Old Lady Vixen. They never caught a glimpse of her (Tony said she must have gotten suspicious and moved), but they saw other animals. At least Tony did. He was always pointing out a chipmunk on a stump, a woodchuck sitting in front of his hole, or a rabbit rummaging in the underbrush. When they were tracking, or just walking, Tony would stop suddenly and tell the Band to listen to the drumming of a woodpecker, or the mating calls of thrushes, sparrows, or warblers, who had just come back from the South. Phoebe could only hear a general twitter, and Constance and Harry, though they'd been instructed by Tony before and wanted to impress him with what they knew, made an awful lot of wrong guesses on birdsongs. Compared to Tony, the Band — all of it, not just Phoebe — was feeble and ignorant.

When Phoebe picked a young skunk cabbage because she thought it was a Jack-in-the-pulpit and got her hands all stinky, everyone laughed at her. But the tables were turned when Constance thought the first marsh marigolds were buttercups. Harry didn't exactly shine in the woods either. Once he was so busy following fox tracks that he almost stepped on a pheasant. It whooshed up right under his nose and scared him so that he let out a howl and sat down hard. That spoiled any chance of finding the vixen that afternoon, but Tony just laughed.

As the Band followed Tony through the woods on one sunny afternoon after another, he began to praise them a little for learning to walk more quietly, or for covering more ground without pooping out. He praised Harry especially for getting faster and stronger and not wheezing so much. Only when someone was careless about exposing himself where he might be seen from a distance, or when Harry and Constance didn't start for home when Tony told them to, did he turn mean. Then his face went stiff and his eyes turned stony, and sometimes he swore at them.

The weekend brought a special dispensation. The Hostile Powers were going to political meetings. They'd be gone all Saturday and Sunday, and Gestapo was driving them. On Saturday morning, Ida put up enough food for lunch and afternoon coffee too. Tony said they'd give up foxes for now and look at hawks. They were back from the South. He had heard them calling.

Tony led the Band off on the longest, roughest hike they had taken yet. Phoebe lost count of the number of times they scrambled to the top of a ridge, slid down the other side, forded the stream in the gully (the snow was melting, and all the brooks were running), and started up all over again. The ridges got higher and wilder the farther they went. Near the top of a particularly savage and windy spur, just below the summit of Old Mott, Tony motioned to them to drop to their knees and crawl the rest of the way to the top. Here the ground dropped off sharply. Lying on their stomachs among the rocks, the twisted trees, and the prickly junipers, they could look straight down on the treetops in the ravine below. Tony pointed and nodded and made signs, but Phoebe could see nothing below but bare branches interspersed with spikes of evergreen. Suddenly, out of nowhere, two big birds swooped down so close that the Band could hear the wind whistling through their wing feathers. The Band hugged the ground; the hawks must not have seen them, for they plunged on down into the ravine and landed in the top of one of the bare trees below. Now at last, Phoebe spotted the nest Tony had been trying to point out, a big, messy bunch of sticks set in a fork just below the spot where the birds had landed. The hawks now spent some time looking over the nest and poking at it with their beaks. Then, at the same instant, both of them took off again and soared high up over the ravine.

Never, even in movies about fighter pilots or in trapeze acts at the circus, had Phoebe seen such acrobatics as the hawks now performed. They spiraled up, dropped, glided, spiraled again, wove over and under each other like dancers, and sometimes flew at each other head-on until, just as they were about to collide, one dropped or swerved in the nick of time, only to spiral away again after his partner in ever faster, wilder flights. All this time they were exchanging screeches so savage that they curdled Phoebe's blood. Gradually the hawks soared higher and higher, until they were two tiny black specks swinging against the sky. Tony kept the Band a long time in silence and considerable discomfort from wind and prickles, waiting for the hawks to come down again, but they never came.

Later, when the Band was sitting around its fire farther down the mountain in a sheltered spot, Tony told them the hawks they had seen were probably Red Tails — and what they had just performed was a mating dance. Those screeches were screeches of love and joy. Sometimes in the course of their mating ceremonies, Tony said, the hawks performed even more extraordinary flying feats than those the Band had just seen, but they

145

usually did these special tricks so high up that you couldn't watch them without strong binoculars.

Tony turned to Phoebe. "Is there a store in Denby that sells good binoculars?"

Phoebe couldn't think of one, but Harry said that Tony could order very good binoculars from one of the sporting-goods catalogues. Phoebe could get him a postal money order for whatever the binoculars cost, mail it with the order, and pick up the parcel at her post office box when it arrived. Tony liked this idea and told Harry to bring up the catalogues next day.

"What made you send for sporting-goods catalogues?" he asked. "You never get to use that sort of stuff, the way they keep you cooped up."

Harry was slow to reply. "I just sent for them because Phoebe had got the box for us, and I wanted to get the good of it."

"That's not true," Constance broke in. "He sent for them so we could pick out equipment to take to Nepal."

Harry glared at her, and Phoebe held her breath, waiting for Tony's wrath to fall, but it didn't. He took out his cigarettes, put them back, sighed, and said, "Don't count on getting to Nepal this year, Con."

"But we've got to, or they'll send us to boarding school in Switzerland, and we'll never see you again."

"Maybe it won't be so bad as that. When I come into my money, maybe I can fix something up, but not Nepal."

"Then what?"

"I don't know. Don't bug me."

"We will go some time, won't we, Tony? We've planned it for so long."

"Sure," said Tony, "but forget it for now. We're having a good time together here, aren't we?" Phoebe noticed how gentle his eyes were now, as he looked at each member of the Band, including her.

"Of course we are," replied Constance, "but — "

"Then just lay off," said Tony.

On Sunday it rained, but the Band didn't care. After they had helped Tony wash up his dirty dishes and haul in a supply of firewood, they sat around the stove in the Secret Place and read the comics, while he looked through the catalogues and decided what kind of binoculars to order. At the end of the day, he sent Phoebe off with an order signed by her with Miranda's signature for the most expensive pair of binoculars in the catalogues, and a wad of money with which she was to buy the postal order to pay for them.

The unseasonably warm weather went on and on. As Phoebe climbed up through the woods, she noticed that the drifts were melting away, that the birches were putting out little green buds and the maples little pink ones. Even the sombre old evergreens were sporting bright yellow needles at the tips of their branches. Higher up, the trail had dried out. The bristly black bushes that Phoebe grabbed onto as she climbed had turned pinky-lavender, and some sprouted pussy willows. More birds arrived every day, and Phoebe began to recognize some of their songs. She heard the Canada Geese honking and watched them fly by in wedge formation, heading north. When she reached the terrace in front of the mine and looked back the way she had come, the old brown winter landscape was all misted over with green.

Every afternoon the Band met in the Nook or the Secret Place, and Tony led them out on new excursions. One afternoon as they were returning from visiting a waterfall, Tony said they would drop down through Slabland on the chance of seeing the fox again, or better still the vixen. The wind was blowing away from Slabland, toward them. The vixen would not catch their scent. They were to walk quietly and not chatter. Luck was with them; before they got into Slabland proper, while they were still hidden in the brush, Tony spotted the vixen. She was sitting on a big flat rock with her orange coat glowing in the sun and her brush flowing out like a train behind her. The four cubs played around her. They were no bigger than kittens, and they pounced, rolled, cuffed at one another, bared their little white teeth, and nipped and snarled in the most spirited manner. Every few minutes the vixen would lift her head, listen with pricked-up ears, and sniff the wind, but she never guessed she was being watched. When she barked at the cubs, and they scuttled off obediently among the rocks, it wasn't because she was alarmed; she was just sending them in after their afternoon romp. She saw that they were safely stowed away, then loped off into the woods.

Tony led the Band a good distance away before he allowed himself or anyone else to exclaim over their good fortune. Constance wished again that she could have a cub for a pet, but Tony said he wouldn't catch one for her even if he could. To catch and imprison such a beautiful wild creature was worse than killing it. It was sentencing it to a living death. Foxes couldn't be tamed. They were too independent and too proud. They fought captivity tooth and nail until they lost hope. Then they pined slowly away and died.

Suddenly Tony looked at the sun. It was late. He had been careless. He swore at himself. They all ran for the edge of the woods above Dreamwold Castle. Luck was with them again. A minute after Constance and Harry slipped in the kitchen door, Phoebe and Tony, watching from the edge of the woods, saw the Fossil ascend the drive.

That Friday, Phoebe stopped at the post office to check her box and found a notice in it that a parcel had come. It was the binoculars. Tony was delighted. All afternoon he rather neglected the Band while he focused on birds. When Harry said the Hostile Powers were going to keep him and Constance busy with them all weekend, Tony didn't seem very disappointed. He said that since there was only one pair of binoculars, the Band wouldn't be missing much, and it was good policy for Harry and Constance to spend some time with the Hostile Powers. It would allay their suspicions, if they had any. He told Phoebe to bring up the Saturday and Sunday papers on Monday. He had enough cigarettes.

[24]

ON SATURDAY MORNING, Phoebe went downtown for groceries and the paper. She hoped to get some new books to take up to the Eagle's Nest, but Mr. Wade was directing traffic right in front of the library, where he would be sure to see her if she went in. Back at the apartment she took some of her old books and a supply of pop and cake up to the Eagle's Nest. Miranda was away for the day, so Phoebe was in no danger of being interrupted, but she couldn't lose herself in her books. The view of Old Mott, instead of invoking pleasant daydreams, made her feel cramped and restless, and the store cake didn't taste good after Ida's and gave her indigestion besides. In the afternoon, she went for a walk, avoiding the town center where Mr. Wade was still on duty. A walk around Denby was pretty tame when you were used to ranging the woods with Tony. Phoebe didn't go very far. In the evening, in desperation, she tried to do some homework. This had the advantage of making her very sleepy. She went to bed without waiting for Miranda to come home.

On Sunday morning, Miranda got up early to go somewhere with Charles. She seemed a little put out to learn that Phoebe would be at home, not off playing with her friends. She said she hated to leave her behind, but she didn't invite her to go along. Miranda heard a horn blow way off somewhere (Phoebe didn't even hear it), and suddenly she was in an awful rush. She hugged and kissed Phoebe and dashed off down the backstairs.

Phoebe washed all the dirty dishes and dusted and swept the apartment. They had let it get into an awful mess. She tried again to do homework, but she was so far behind in everything that it seemed hopeless to try to catch up. She walked downtown and bought the Sunday *Globe* and more pop. After that, she just sat and drank pop and read the comics and wished it were time for Miranda to come home.

By midafternoon she was so bored that she was actually glad when Miss Tarlton called "Yoohoo" from the stairwell. Phoebe went to meet her. She was all gussied up in her Sunday best, complete with new spring hat and white gloves, and she shot quick, nosy looks up and down the hall.

"I just wondered if Charles, that is Mr. Tarlton, was here."

"No," said Phoebe.

"Then perhaps Mrs. Smith knows where he is. They are such good friends. I thought she might . . ." Miss Tarlton trailed off.

"They went away together early this morning," said Phoebe, "in his car."

"Oh dear!" All the starch seemed to go out of Miss Tarlton. "He never said anything about that to me." She looked down at her gloves and pulled at them and twisted them until they were all rumpled. She looked up again at Phoebe. "He promised to be here at three to take me to the Historical Society Annual Tea, and Mrs. Smith was invited too, and it's three now, and he hasn't come."

"Maybe he forgot."

"Oh no! He wouldn't do that. I'm afraid he's had an accident." She bit her lip. Her voice trembled.

Phoebe began to feel sorry for her. "It's more likely his car broke down."

"Do you really think so?"

"Yes," said Phoebe. "If he'd had an accident, you'd have been notified by the police."

"Of course. How clever you are! I never thought of that! I know I am foolish, but now that Charles is leaving so soon on that long plane trip back to Japan, I worry about him all the time. He tells me I should wait until he gets on the plane to start worrying, and he is right, of course, but the anxiety is always with me. Here!" Miss Tarlton dabbed at herself with the gloves where her bosom should have been, but where Phoebe could see no sign of it. "You have made me feel so much better," said Miss Tarlton. "I am very grateful to you."

Phoebe was happy to hear that Mr. Charles Tarlton was soon to leave, and Miss Tarlton's gratitude to her was quite touching. Perhaps the old lady wasn't so bad after all. "I'm sure he's all right," she said in a soothing voice.

Miss Tarlton came a step closer and spoke confidentially. "You know how I give up all my Monday, Wednesday, and Friday mornings to the Denby Historical Society, even though I have so many other demands on my time." Phoebe didn't know, but she nodded as if she did. "For years I've given those three mornings from nine to one, with never a break, and I don't just sit there and wait for visitors who want to be shown around. I sweep and dust to save the Society having to hire a cleaning woman, and I take great pains to study up on all our acquisitions. I've been able to prove that a number of the articles the Society wanted to buy weren't genuine. Strictly between you and me and the bedpost, I know more about our collection than Mr. Bartlett, even though he is supposed to be such an authority and is always elected president of the board."

Miss Tarlton bent closer to Phoebe and lowered her voice. "I have had reason to believe that my work wasn't appreciated, that, in fact, I wasn't liked or wanted." She blinked at Phoebe, jerked her head, and set her mouth in a smile. "No doubt I have been overly sensitive, because today, at the Annual Tea, I am to be presented with an award. Mr. Bartlett told me ahead of time so I could prepare my acceptance speech, and when I told Charles about it, he insisted, then and there, that he would drive me to the tea, and that nothing would make him prouder and happier than to watch me get my award and hear me make my speech. He said he was so proud of me that he was going to ask Mrs. Smith to come too, although she is not a regular member, so that she'd realize what a clever old aunt he had. Those were his very words." Miss Tarlton almost giggled, then her chin trembled, and she looked as if she might cry. "It was only a few days ago that he said it, and that is why I am so worried. I am sure he wouldn't forget."

Phoebe wasn't so sure. She thought it would be just

like Mr. Charles Tarlton to take Miranda off gallivanting and forget all about his old aunt. She distinctly remembered that Miranda hadn't said anything about being home by three. Phoebe wouldn't have minded telling Miss Tarlton this, if she had thought it would dim the great Charles's glory, but she was pretty sure it wouldn't. It would just make Miss Tarlton more unhappy.

She decided to develop the breakdown theory instead. "When your car breaks down on Sunday," she said, as if she knew exactly what she was talking about, "it's very hard to get it fixed. Sometimes, in the country, you can't even find a telephone to call a garage."

Miss Tarlton jumped at this. "Of course," she cried, "and that is why Charles hasn't telephoned to tell me he would be late."

Down below, the old clock creaked, bonged once, and was silent.

"Half-past three!" Miss Tarlton caught her breath and made another little dab with her gloves at where her bosom should have been. "I can't wait any longer. I shall have to call Mr. Bartlett and ask him to stop by for me after all. When he offered, I told him Charles was driving me." She bit her lip. "I had so looked forward to going with Charles. Somehow he makes me feel like a queen." She sighed, then lifted her chin and resumed her smile. "Charles's car has broken down in the country. It is too late to walk, and there is no taxi. I must telephone Mr. Bartlett at once."

She started for the stairs, then lingered a moment and looked back as if she hoped Phoebe might come up

154

with some better solution. Her usually cold blue eyes brimmed with sadness and, Phoebe suspected, tears.

Phoebe's heart went out to her. She longed to say, "Wait a minute, Miss Tarlton. I will drive you. I know how, and the keys to the Goldfinch are right here on the table." How happy she would make poor Miss Tarlton, and what a wonderful way of speeding up this interminable afternoon!

She stopped herself just in time. It would never do. It would just make trouble.

She said, "I hope you have a good time at the party, Miss Tarlton, and I'm glad you are getting an award."

"Thank you so much, my dear, you've been a great help." With her smile bravely set, Miss Tarlton disappeared down the stairwell.

It was almost five when Miranda came in. Her face was flushed, and her eyes were puffy as if she had been crying. She said that nothing had gone right all day. In the middle of the afternoon, Charles had remembered that he'd promised to take his aunt to some tea party, and he'd gone wild. The way he drove back, you'd think he'd left his Aunt Grace tied to the railroad track and had to get her off before the Three-Thirty Express squashed her flat, and all the time he scolded at Miranda because she hadn't reminded him. As if it was her business to remind him of his engagements! He sounded as if he cared more for his old aunt than he did for Miranda, and Miranda was beginning to think maybe he did.

At this point, Miranda almost cried, but she blew her nose and swallowed a few times and said that Charles

had been going to take her and Phoebe out to dinner —
a sort of farewell dinner, because he was leaving so soon.
She swallowed again. Now, though, he was taking Miss
Tarlton to dinner, to make up for forgetting her. Miranda hoped Phoebe could cook up something for herself.
Miranda couldn't eat a thing, and she was tired, and she
had a big bunch of papers to correct besides. She went
into her room and shut the door, and stayed there. She
didn't even come out to kiss Phoebe good night.

[25]

ON MONDAY, all dreariness vanished in the sunshine and
the excitement of following Tony on another adventure. He took the Band back to Hawk Ridge and let
them watch the hawks through his binoculars. There
were four eggs in the nest now, and the parents took
turns sitting on them. When the guard changed, the re-
lieving sitter swooped in at such speed that Phoebe
expected the old sitter to be knocked galley west and all
the eggs to be smashed, but in the nick of time the old
sitter took off, and the new one landed as lightly as a
chickadee.

The next afternoon, they went to Hidden Pond,
which was very well hidden in the middle of a swamp
and all a-twitter and a-flutter with birds building their
nests. While Tony watched the birds through his binoculars, the Band tried to catch the turtles that were out

sunning themselves along the water's edge. They crept up like cats and pounced, but the turtles always slipped off their logs or rocks into the water before anyone could quite lay hands on one of them. The Band got muddier and wetter, until it didn't really matter whether they fell in all the way or not, and Harry did fall in and then pretended to be The Creature from the Black Lagoon and chased the girls, making horrible noises and throwing mud. Tony told him to quit and shut up because he was frightening the birds, but Tony himself was laughing so hard that he could hardly talk. They dried Harry off in the sun and by a fire which Phoebe built and lit with one match. Harry didn't even get a sniffle, and the next day Tony said that since all of them, especially Harry, were in such good shape, they could try some rock climbing at Lama's Leap. Constance jumped up and down.

"It's what I've wanted to do right along," she cried, "but I was afraid to say so because you'd think I was bugging you about Nepal." Tony laughed.

He led them off in the direction of Hawk Ridge (Phoebe was beginning to know her way around now, not so well as Tony of course, but as well as Constance and Harry) to another narrow ravine with a steep rock wall at its head. The wall went straight up and looked as forbidding and unscalable as the walls of Tibetan lamaseries Phoebe had seen in books. Tony pointed out that it was pitted with cracks and crevices and traversed by wide ledges. You could climb to the very top, and Tony did so, but he wouldn't let the Band go beyond the first ledge. All afternoon, they scrambled around, finding new routes up new cracks, new hand and foot holds, new ways of using them. Tony watched and encouraged, and gave advice and never once got impatient or mean.

"This is how it will be in Nepal," Constance shouted, as she sat on the ledge, swinging her legs and grinning.

"It'll be better," Tony shouted back, "but you've got to improve your technique. Now heave yourself onto that ledge again and use your feet, not your knees."

Before Phoebe went home that night, Tony commissioned her to buy two fifty-foot lengths of seven-sixteenth inch nylon rope.

The next afternoon, Tony climbed with one rope up to the second ledge and tied himself to a fir tree that had taken root there. Next, he passed the rope once around his own waist and dropped the free end to each member of the Band in turn. Each member in turn tied himself into the rope with a bowline (Tony had drilled them in the knot before they started) and, with Tony and the rope to stop him if he fell, climbed up to the second ledge. This was "belaying." After Tony had belayed the Band to the second ledge, he belayed them on, one by one, to the very top of the wall and down again. Later, using both ropes, he taught them to belay each other from above, and then to do continuous climbing and belay from below as well.

For the next few days, scaling and belaying one another up and down Lama's Leap absorbed all the energies of the Band. Climbing called up every bit of concentration and guts they possessed. It taxed their muscle, wind, and agility, and all the discipline and patience they had learned from their forays with Tony. It beat "When the Cat's Away" hollow, and it was for real. It seemed to

Phoebe, as she put her faith in her rope, her belayer, and her skill, and scrambled up the exposed rock or as she manned a belay for a comrade, that now, indeed, they were all for one and one for all, as she had dreamed they would be in Nepal, and that, at last, she was a full-fledged member of Tony's Band.

Meanwhile the fine weather and Tony's good mood continued. As they traveled to and from Lama's Leap, Tony took pains to point out a pair of phoebe birds to Phoebe and to let her get a good look at them through the binoculars, so she'd be sure to know the bird she was named for. He uncovered the first mayflowers under the dead leaves and waited while Constance picked a bunch to take home to Ida. He sometimes let Harry carry the binoculars when they were in the vicinity of Slabland, so he could scan the landscape for foxes; and once Harry actually did spot Old Foxy trotting along in the direction of Big Slab, perhaps to pay a visit to his family.

On Friday, Tony found a new cliff for them to climb and took no offense when Constance named it "Lhotse Face."

They were dispersed over the Lhotse Face, so absorbed in their climbing that no one noticed the first few snowflakes that blew down from the top of Old Mott. Suddenly the few flakes had become a horde, swooping in on blasts of wind so savage that they almost tore the climbers from their perches. Phoebe latched on to the nearest good hand and foot holds. The sun went out, and a moment later she was swallowed up in a maelstrom of whirling snow. The wind whistled through her light clothing and chilled her to the bone. The snow lashed

159

and stung and in a few moments had deposited treacherous icy slime over her and the shelf of rock to which she clung. She dared not move an inch for fear of slipping. She called out and heard the others calling from somewhere in the gray mass of snowflakes, which was all she could see. What they said was drowned out by the wind. Her hands especially began to ache with cold, but she didn't dare loosen her grip on the rock to flex her fingers or shake the snow off them. She clung to her perch, as helpless, miserable, and scared as if she had been clinging to the real Lhotse Face while a Himalayan blizzard raged. Suddenly the wind dropped. The gray mass of snowflakes thinned out, the landscape showed through, and the sun came out. The storm had lasted about ten minutes, but that was quite long enough.

Under Tony's direction, the Band climbed shakily down from their various perches.

They built a big fire right at the foot of Lhotse Face and gathered around it, shivering partly from cold and lingering fear, but even more from elation at having been caught up in danger and come through unscathed. As they drank hot coffee and wolfed down slices of Ida's fruitcake, they all talked at once, telling each other how they had felt up there and what they thought, and they all wondered aloud what would have happened if the blizzard had continued. Although Tony laughed at them and assured them that he'd have gotten them down safely, he, too, seemed excited and talked about blizzards he'd been out in on Old Mott when he was a kid, and how cold and scared he had been. Phoebe, feeling truly one of the Band, described her favorite blizzard for Tony, the one

Tenzing and Lambert had sat through in their tent on the South Face of Everest. For a minute, after she had finished, she was afraid Tony might think that now *she* was bugging him and get angry again. He didn't. Instead he described the blizzard that had swallowed Norton and Mallory, the greatest climber of them all, on the Northeast Summit Ridge of Everest in 1924.

"I wish I could read Mallory's letters again, and the articles he wrote," said Tony. "They were the best things I ever read."

"Phoebe can get them for you out of the library," said Harry.

"Can you?" Tony turned to Phoebe.

"Sure," said Phoebe, and then she remembered Mr. Wade. "Only —"

"Only what?"

Phoebe dropped her head. She hated to bring up Mr. Wade now after avoiding him so carefully and not mentioning him for so long.

"You used to get books all the time," said Constance. "What's the matter?"

"It's Mr. Wade," muttered Phoebe.

"You mean the old policeman in Denby?" Tony took her up. "Is he still around? What about him?"

Phoebe had no choice. She explained how she used to talk to Mr. Wade every day when she came out of the library, and how, long before she knew Tony, Mr. Wade had talked about him and his hide-out on the mountain, and had invited her to go up to the Old Tin Mine with him in the spring so they could look at the view and poke around and look for Tony's hide-out, and how

161

she had avoided Mr. Wade ever since Tony came back because she was afraid that, if Mr. Wade saw her, he'd want to take her up to the tin mine, especially since the weather was so warm and springlike, and she knew Tony wouldn't want that; but, if Mr. Wade insisted, she didn't know how she could get out of it without making Mr. Wade suspicious, he being a grownup and a policeman. He directed traffic right outside the library every afternoon and all day Saturday, and the library was closed nights and Sundays.

Tony didn't answer her at once. He scowled at the fire.

"Wade's just an old windbag," put in Harry. "Phoebe shouldn't believe what he says, and you needn't worry about him, Tony. He'd never find the Secret Place, even if he could climb that far, which he can't because he's too old."

"Don't be so sure," said Tony. "He used to be a fast climber, and he knows his way around the mountain. He almost found me once or twice in the old days." Tony paused and sighed. "When they used to take me down to the station house to make me confess to all the things I'd done, it was Wade who asked the hard questions. Once or twice, I almost did confess because of him. Phoebe's right to stay clear of him. I don't want to tangle with him now. I don't want any trespassers around, least of all him. No one must know I'm here. Remember that." Tony sighed again. "I wish I could get hold of those books though."

"I can get my tutor to look them up and order them," said Harry.

"That's a good idea," Tony brightened.

"I'll tell my tutor I want the books for myself. He believes everything I tell him, and Tony, the Hostile Powers are going away again tomorrow. So can we come up for the whole day again? It's perfectly safe, and you don't know how dull it is when we can't come."

"O.K.," said Tony. "We'll practice falling with the ropes, and maybe I'll teach you to rappel."

The snow had all melted when they started home. The woods were full of birdsongs, and the spring greenery shone fresher and brighter than ever after the storm.

[26]

ON SATURDAY MORNING, Phoebe awoke to sunshine and a glorious feeling of anticipation. The very sound of the word *rappel* — she wasn't sure what it meant — excited her. She said it over to herself as she dressed and could hardly wait to be off. Miranda came into the kitchen while Phoebe was stuffing down her corn flakes.

"He's gone," said Miranda. "He's gone back to Japan. He never really loved me, and I've been such a fool." She sank into a chair beside Phoebe, threw her arms around Phoebe's neck, and burst into tears.

Phoebe hadn't seen Miranda so down in the dumps since long ago, after Phil was killed. Then Charlotte had been on hand to help with the comforting. Now Phoebe felt terribly awkward and inadequate as she stroked Miranda's hair, patted her shoulder, and begged her not to cry.

At length Miranda lifted her head, groped for a Kleenex, which Phoebe handed her, blew her nose and blurted out, still half sobbing, "He has a wife — a sort of wife — in Japan. He doesn't talk about her much here because she isn't a Christian, and his aunt doesn't think he is properly married to her, and he wouldn't do anything to upset his aunt." Miranda sniffed. "When he talked to me about her he never said right out that he was married to her. He says he thought I understood because I was intelligent and enlightened, and I did in a way, at first, that is; but later, I didn't want to understand. I pretended to myself that Akiko — that's her name — was really just a sort of servant, and that Charles would marry me." Miranda laid her head on the kitchen table and sobbed anew. In vain, Phoebe patted her, stroked her, and implored her to stop. Finally she put her mouth close to Miranda's ear.

"You shouldn't cry about Mr. Tarlton. He's selfish and stuck-up. You're much too good for him, and I'm glad he's gone away."

Miranda lifted her head. "He's no more selfish and stuck-up than I am, and he did love me in a way, and it wasn't his fault I misunderstood him. It was my own fault. I was a fool." Again the sobs overcame her.

"No, no, Miranda!" cried Phoebe. Miranda went on sobbing.

At her wit's end, Phoebe bent close to Miranda's ear again. "If you'd married him, I would have left you."

Miranda reached out, clutched Phoebe's hand, and

sobbed harder than ever. Phoebe's own eyes filled with tears. She wiped them away, glanced up at the clock, and even while her heart ached for Miranda, she noted that if she couldn't get away soon, she would be late for the rendezvous at the Old Mine. Shame at her own selfishness overwhelmed her. She laid her head on the table beside Miranda's and, with renewed devotion, whispered every endearing and comforting word she knew. All the time, she also knew in her heart that she was making this effort for herself as much as for Miranda. The kitchen clock went on ticking, and Miranda went on sobbing. At last Miranda raised her head again, let go of Phoebe's hand, gave her nose an especially determined blow, wiped her red, swollen eyes, and said quite steadily, "I've learned my lesson. I'm not the heroine of a romance. No prince is going to carry me away to the land of dreams. I'm just a poor, working schoolteacher, but I'm independent, and I have you, Phoebe. You're worth a thousand Charleses, but I've neglected you. I haven't been a good mother to you." Miranda looked as if she might start crying again.

"Yes, you have," cried Phoebe.

Miranda shook her head. "I've neglected Charlotte too. Next to you, she is the dearest thing I have, and I've hardly thought of her for months. I'm so ashamed of myself."

"Don't be," cried Phoebe. "Charlotte won't mind."

Miranda smiled faintly and again she took Phoebe's hand. "I haven't been looking after you properly. We must have a long talk."

Even while she loathed herself, Phoebe couldn't help

glancing up at the clock. Then she couldn't bear to look at Miranda. Miranda didn't say anything for a minute, then she let go of Phoebe's hand and patted it.

"I've kept you long enough. I'm sure you have plans to play with your friends. It's a beautiful day. Run along."

To her shame, Phoebe felt her heart leap for joy. "Are you sure you don't mind?" She still couldn't look Miranda in the face.

"Of course not, dear. We'll have our talk later. I've lots to do. First I'll write to Charlotte, then I'll get out my thesis and look it over and start thinking about finishing it. I've neglected it, too."

"Then I'll start along."

"Will you be home for lunch? I might bake a cake or something."

Phoebe went on staring straight in front of her. "Constance and some other kids and I were going on a picnic. Constance has the food all ready."

"How nice," said Miranda. "I'll expect you for supper, then. Run along."

Phoebe made herself look at Miranda and smile. Miranda smiled back bravely, all too bravely. Phoebe longed to hug and kiss her, but she was afraid Miranda might cling to her again and start crying. She blew her a kiss instead.

"See you at supper," she called, and feeling guilty as sin she ran down the backstairs and away.

[27]

ALL THE TIME she was sneaking through town doing her errands, Phoebe went on feeling guilty; but once she got on the mountain, with the birds twittering all around and the sun shining slantwise through the new green leaves, Miranda and her troubles began to slip away. Phoebe climbed her fastest, but even so when she clambered onto the terrace, she was scarcely out of breath. She smiled to remember how exhausted she had been the first time she climbed up to meet Tony. Now she was almost as strong and nimble as he was, and a true member of his Band besides. She whistled. Tony appeared. He had the binoculars in his hand and motioned her to wait. He was stalking a bird. It fluttered into a tree just below them. After Tony had taken a good look at it, he took the newspaper and cigarettes from Phoebe and handed her the binoculars. The bird was a Redstart, he said. She should look at it carefully and learn to distinguish it from an oriole.

Phoebe was trying to sight the bird in the binoculars when she heard a cry from below.

"Skibootch! Hey, Skibootch!"

There down on the trail stood Ben Barker. She knew him at once. He waved his arms. "Skibootch," he called again. "Skibootch!"

The binoculars dropped from Phoebe's hands. She heard the glass shatter on the terrace, then the thud as they bounced into the underbrush. She dove behind the nearest boulder. Tony was already there.

"Who's that?"

Phoebe couldn't speak for fear.

"Who?"

"I don't know," she managed to say.

"Skibootch!" The cry welled up and sank slowly into the stillness.

Tony cursed. He grabbed Phoebe's hand and yanked her after him, dodging from boulder to boulder, until they jumped down into the Nook. Harry and Constance crouched there listening.

"Who's that calling?" asked Harry.

"I don't know. I couldn't see that far," said Tony. He gave Phoebe a mean look. "She broke my binoculars." His look got meaner. "Are you sure you haven't blabbed about coming up here? Are you sure you haven't been blabbing to Wade?"

"I'm sure," said Phoebe. She was happy to be able to tell this much truth.

Tony glared at Constance and Harry. "What about you? Have you kept your mouths shut?"

"Of course we have," said Harry.

Nearer and clearer, the call sounded again. "Skibootch! Hi there, Skibootch!"

"He's not calling any of us," said Harry. "It's some funny name."

"There must be two of them," whispered Tony. "I'm getting my gun."

"Keep your shirt on," said Harry. "Maybe this

168

guy who's calling is just climbing the mountain with his friend with the funny name — Skootch, or whatever — and they got separated, and the guy saw you and thought it was Skootch."

"Dry up," said Tony. "We're getting into the Secret Place before he walks in on top of us. Pick up the gear. Hurry."

They grabbed up jackets, the knapsack, ropes, and the empty binocular case. Tony led them on hands and knees in and out between boulders to a tunnel opening, and they crawled through that tunnel into another which at length brought them into the Secret Place. Tony lighted candles, doused the fire in the stove, went into one of the alcoves, and came back with his pistol and holster. Harry planted himself in front of him.

"You don't need that, Tony. If you shoot anyone, you'll just be in worse trouble."

"I'll worry about that," said Tony. "All of you wait here and be quiet." He strapped the holster under his arm and climbed up the ladder out of sight.

The Band gathered around the stove, which still had a little warmth in it, and waited in obedient silence. Phoebe had time to think about the awful thing she had done. When she should have been one for all and all for one, she had lied to Tony about Ben. But she hadn't done it deliberately. She'd done it out of fear. How could she, she asked herself, admit that Ben was calling her, when all the time Tony was glaring at her, and when she had just broken his binoculars? Besides, she would have to tell him how she and Ben had trespassed before, and how she had kept quiet about it. To tell Tony all that, when he was mad already, was more than she could do, and she didn't think Constance or Harry would have dared to either. She wondered if she should explain to them now and let them explain to Tony. She glanced at Constance, who had begun to pace up and down, muttering under her breath and tossing her head. Harry stood motionless, wheezing a little, scowling at the stove. She knew she didn't dare tell them. They'd join up with Tony to drive her away in disgrace. She knew she must just keep quiet and hope that Ben had gone away and wouldn't get shot, and that Tony would quiet down and she wouldn't be found out. A shivering seized her. She crouched over the stove, but it gave almost no heat now. Constance paced, Harry scowled. It got colder and colder. Phoebe shivered harder. Finally Tony came back down the ladder.

"Well?" asked Harry.

"He's gone back down."

"Was he anyone you'd ever seen before?"

"I don't think so. I couldn't get close enough to be sure. If I'd had the binoculars — " For a minute his eyes rested on Phoebe, cold and hard and mean. He snatched the newspaper off the table where he had left it, opened it to the advertising section, and scanned the columns. "Nothing," he said, "as usual." He scrunched the paper in his fist and dropped it.

"What about the guy the other guy was calling — Skootch or whatever his name is?"

"No sign of him. I scouted all around." Tony sat down and lit a cigarette.

"If there's nobody around," said Constance, "let's get started for Lhotse Face."

Tony jumped up. "For chrissake!" he shouted, "don't you think about anything but your games?" The glare he gave Constance seemed to Phoebe even worse than the ones he had given her. Constance shrank back.

"Keep your shirt on," said Harry. "She doesn't understand."

"None of you understands," retorted Tony. His voice broke. "You're just kids."

Harry laid his hand on Tony's arm. "I do. I have right along."

Tony dropped the cigarette and stamped on it. He looked down at Harry. His eyes softened. His mouth twisted into a little smile. "You always did have the brains. I've got to know who came up here trespassing. Tell me how I can find out?"

"You keep your shirt on," said Harry, "and wait for Phoebe to find out for you."

"Phoebe!" Tony's voice rose hard and scornful.

Harry went on calmly. "Phoebe will go down to that policeman friend of hers, Mr. Wade, the one you say knows so much, and she'll get him talking and find out if he's heard anything about you, or if you're wanted for anything. If the cops are after you, he'll know, and he loves to talk."

"Cops!" exclaimed Constance.

"Shut up!" said Tony with another glare. He turned back to Harry. "How's Phoebe supposed to do that? He doesn't have to tell her anything. She'll just make him suspicious."

"It's a chance we've got to take," replied Harry. "He trusts her. Didn't he tell her all about you before? She'll get him to talk about you again." Harry turned to Phoebe. "O.K.?"

"I c-c-can't," cried Phoebe between chattering teeth.

"Of course you can," said Harry. "You've lied to old Wade plenty of times before. You can do it again for Tony's sake."

"T-Tony said I was to stay away from Mr. Wade."

"Don't make excuses," said Harry. "This is an emergency."

"What if she messes it up?" asked Tony.

"If you can think of any other way to find out what you've got to know, let's hear it," retorted Harry.

Tony swore, glared at Phoebe, and said, "All right, come on."

"B-but, what do I do?" Phoebe's teeth were chattering so she could hardly speak.

"I told you," said Harry. "You go down to your friend Mr. Wade and get him to talk about Tony. You know how to lead him on. Find out if he's heard anything new about Tony lately and get him to tell you all about it."

"B-but — "

"You've got to do it. You can't get out of it. Not if you're a member of the Band." Harry smiled, and his smile struck Phoebe as neither friendly nor encouraging. It was a threat.

"Come on!" Tony gestured Phoebe to follow him. She did, through several tunnels — until they came out into the sunshine on the mountainside.

"Go straight down," said Tony, "until you hit the Tarlton Trail. You'll know it. Don't bother to whistle when you come back. I'll be watching for you."

[28]

PHOEBE HAD NO IDEA where she was. The sunlight blinded her, and she was still shaking so hard that she fell several times and scraped herself. Her eyes were filled with tears, blinding her even more. She wanted to sit down and cry, but she knew that Tony was watching her, so she kept groping her way down. At last she hit the trail, and the going got easier. Gradually her eyes became accustomed to the light, and the sun and exercise warmed her, and she began to be glad she was outdoors instead of in the Secret Place with no fire and Tony turned mean.

Tony hadn't been mean like this since he first came. Just because a trespasser happened to see him from a distance wasn't any reason for him to glare so, and curse out his Band, and grab his gun as if the cops were on his tail. What was he so scared of, anyway? Certainly not the Evil Eye! Phoebe stopped in her tracks. Maybe the cops really were after him! Maybe he had done something bad before he came, and that was why he came early without warning Constance and Harry! He had been scared then the way he was now. Maybe the newspaper he had to have every day was supposed to tell him something, but it never did. With increasing dread, Phoebe began to understand what she and Constance had been too dumb to understand before. No wonder Tony had yelled at them. No wonder Harry had threatened her. He had known right along that Tony was in trouble with the cops. That was why he was making Phoebe go off now to find out what Mr. Wade knew.

Terror seized Phoebe. What if Ben had stopped to talk to Mr. Wade on his way back through town and told him about seeing Phoebe and a strange man up at the Old Mine? Mightn't that be just the tip the cops needed to find Tony? Phoebe began to run. She was going to have to lie as she never had before, if she was to save Tony and redeem herself.

She ran all the way to the end of town. From there she could see Mr. Wade in his circle at the far end of the business block, directing traffic as usual. She decided to start off by telling him she had been sick, and that was why she hadn't been by to see him. After that, she would have to put her faith in her own wits and Mr. Wade's fondness for talking.

She took a quick look up and down the business block and made sure that Ben's red-white-and-blue taxi wasn't among the cars parked on either side of the road. The last person she wanted to meet right now was Ben. As she figured it, Ben had climbed to the Old Mine in order to give Charlotte and Miranda a chance to have what Charlotte called a gab fest. By now, he'd be back at the apartment, or maybe — and Phoebe felt a twinge of envy — driving Charlotte and Miranda to lunch at the Mottrell Arms on the other side of town. There would be one vacant chair at the table, and Phoebe wished with all her heart that she was in it, a Stebbins Girl again, with no secrets and no need ever to tell a lie.

She swept the scene from her mind. She had her work to do. She tossed her head as Constance did, felt her eyes flash, and walked boldly toward Mr. Wade. She didn't need her opening gambit.

He called, "Hey there, Phoebe Smith. I want to talk to you." He left his traffic circle and walked over to her on the sidewalk. "Your friend Mr. Ben Barker stopped by a little while ago. He said he saw you up in front of the Old Tin Mine. I told him it couldn't be you, and I hope I was right."

"I'd never go up there alone," exclaimed Phoebe with a great show of righteousness. "You told me not to."

Mr. Wade gave her an approving nod. "That's what I told Mr. Barker, and I told him you were the one kid I'd trust, and now I want you to promise me that for the next day or two when you take your walks, you'll stay out of the woods around Old Mott."

Phoebe tried to make her eyes very round and innocent. "Why?" she asked.

"Never mind why. It's a nasty business, and nothing a nice kid like you needs to know about. You just promise." Mr. Wade looked severe.

Phoebe promised. "Who do you think Ben did see up on the mountain?" she went on, doing her best to keep up the wide-eyed-innocence look.

"I don't think," replied Mr. Wade. "I know, and I know why that person was up there too, but I didn't tell any of this to Mr. Barker."

Phoebe gathered all her courage. She must bring

Mr. Wade to the point. "Does what Ben saw have anything to do with that boy you told me about, the one that was always getting into trouble and loved Old Mott so much he couldn't stay away for long? You said he had a hide-out up near the mine, and he'd come back to it. Remember?" She frowned and rubbed her forehead as if she were trying to remember something. Her boldness astonished her, and Mr. Wade snapped up the bait.

"You've got a good memory," he said. "That's the one, Tony Mottrell, and he's in trouble again."

Phoebe's heart was thumping so loudly she wondered that Mr. Wade couldn't hear it too. "What did he do?" she managed to get out between the thumps.

Mr. Wade frowned and shook his head. She was sure she had gone too fast and made him suspicious, but after a long moment he heaved a sigh and said, "Since I told you so much about Tony already, I guess there's no harm in telling you more. I know I can trust you not to spread it around, and I'll feel better if I talk about it to someone. They're so set against him. Everyone is against him, even his own father."

"I'm not," said Phoebe. It was always a relief, if only for a moment, to be able to tell the truth.

"That's what I mean," said Mr. Wade, and then he just looked off over Phoebe's head and scowled for so long she wondered if she was going to have to prod him again to get him going. "If there was any way I could stop the hullabaloo, I would," he exclaimed.

"What hullabaloo?" ventured Phoebe.

"The special agents, the dogs, the helicopter!" Mr. Wade made a disgusted gesture.

"What are they for?"

"To catch Tony."

"What did he do?"

"He killed a man."

"Oh no!" cried Phoebe from her heart. "Not Tony!" and she was almost paralyzed for fear that she had given herself away. Mr. Wade, however, was too taken up with his own thoughts to notice.

"He didn't mean to," he said. "He was hasty, as usual. This is what happened, as I understand it. Tony and a young fellow with a record and a list of aliases as long as my arm — right now he calls himself Rick Shaw — robbed a bank in Oneida, New York. They lined up the employees and the customers, and Tony held a pistol on them while Rick emptied the cash drawers. Rick was skillful. He had pulled lots of jobs like this before. They were all set to go, clean and nice, when Tony's trigger finger got nervous. His pistol went off, and the bullet hit the president of the bank in the leg." Mr. Wade sighed. "They made their getaway then and divided the money. Rick went to hide out with his girl friend in the next town until the excitement blew over, but they got him the next day because the girl squealed on him. She was paid to. Tony came back here. The local police there tried to find him in a halfhearted way, but they didn't even know his right name, and they didn't have any information on him because it was his first criminal offense. The police had just about given up on finding him, when the bank president, who had been doing fine, got a blood clot and died. He was an important man with political connections. The FBI was called in to find who had killed him. They had ways of finding out who Tony was and tracking him to Denby.

"When the agents came around a few days ago to talk to me, I told them I could find Tony for them and bring him back alive. They didn't like that idea at all. They said he was dangerous and armed, and they'd have to get together some more agents, and the dogs, and the helicopter before they'd even let me show them where Tony was. The helicopter should be in by this afternoon, and they've sent to Boston for the dogs."

"When will they start after him?" asked Phoebe.

"I can't be sure," said Mr. Wade, "but I doubt they'll get all the paraphernalia together before tomorrow morning, and I won't let them start until I'm sure that little sister of Tony's is safe at home."

"His little sister?" Phoebe was genuinely puzzled.

"She's the one your friend Mr. Barker saw up there with Tony and thought was you. You're about the same size," said Mr. Wade knowingly.

"What was his little sister doing up there?" asked Phoebe.

"I expect she brings him clothes and food and things he needs from the house. They're so rich they'd never miss anything. There's a brother too, but he's an invalid. He doesn't get out much. The sister's a handsome, strong girl, with a bold light in her eye. I've seen her go by in the limousine. She reminds me of Tony. She wouldn't turn against her brother, or be afraid to help him out of

178

a jam. I'd bet on her to stand up to Mr. Henry Mottrell himself." Mr. Wade paused and wrinkled his nose in distaste. "I've got to go up to see him tonight to explain about what's going to happen tomorrow and to make sure he keeps his daughter in the house until the hullabaloo is over. I don't want to talk to him, and I don't want to show those agents up to the Old Mine either. If it wasn't my duty to uphold the law, I'd warn Tony to get out while there's still time. I knew him when he was just a little fellow, and he's not all bad. If I'd studied my books and become a preacher, the way Mother wanted me to, I could be helping Tony now, instead of hunting him down." Mr. Wade settled himself comfortably with his back against the big old tree. Phoebe recognized the storytelling light in his eye.

"I've got to go home," she exclaimed. If she let him get started, he might go on talking until the dogs and the helicopter arrived.

"Of course you do." Mr. Wade smiled his kindly smile. "When an old fellow like me gets talking — "

"Good-bye," shouted Phoebe, at her wit's end, and she set off at a run back toward the business block.

"Aren't you going in the wrong direction?" called Mr. Wade after her. "Unless you've moved — "

Phoebe stopped, and her heart seemed to stop too. At the last minute, had she ruined everything?

"What's the matter?" asked Mr. Wade.

"I've been sick," gasped Phoebe. "I haven't been out for a long time. I get mixed up and dizzy."

Mr. Wade regarded her closely. She was sure he didn't believe her, but after a minute he said, "So, that's why I haven't seen you around for so long. You do look kind of pale. You get along home, but walk slowly, don't wear yourself out. If you feel faint, just sit down on the curb and put your head between your knees. When the hullabaloo is over, and you've got your strength back, we'll go up to the Old Mine together. I haven't forgotten my promise."

"Thank you," murmured Phoebe.

She walked very slowly past the library to the alley behind the post office. There she stopped as if to rest, but really to look behind her. Mr. Wade was in his circle again. His back was to her. She nipped down the alley and through the business block by her usual back way. As soon as she was out of town, she began to run. She ran through the woods, and up through the scrub and boulders, and was still running when Tony reached out from behind a bush and pulled her off the trail, led her through more scrub into a tunnel, and through the tunnel into the Secret Place.

[29]

TONY TURNED on Phoebe. "Was it the cops?"

"No, I mean yes," panted Phoebe.

"Come on, make sense! Who was the guy calling? Who was Skootch?"

"They don't matter," cried Phoebe, fighting for breath, "because the cops are coming tomorrow with dogs and a helicopter, and oh Tony, they're going to get you and take you off to jail!" Phoebe's knees gave way. She sank to the ground and began to sob.

"Now you've scared her so you'll never get any sense out of her," she heard Harry say.

Tony swore. Then he helped her up, led her to a chair, and offered her his handkerchief. Harry and Constance began to bustle around. Constance produced leftovers from lunch. Harry draped a blanket over Phoebe's shoulders. They all stood and watched her while she mastered her sobbing and took a few bites of sandwich and deviled egg. Constance and Harry were bundled up in old clothes of Tony's, and Phoebe huddled down into her blanket, for already the chill was creeping over her. Shakily, she began her story. Tony interrupted to swear. Harry interrupted to ask questions and get things straight. When she had finished, Tony squared his shoulders and tossed his head. His eyes gleamed in the candlelight.

"I'll wait for them here, and I'll get some of them before they get me." He patted the place under his arm where his pistol hung. "I'll pay them back for what they did to Rick."

"Forget it," said Harry.

"Shut up," returned Tony. "You may be a brain, but you don't know everything. Rick could have squealed on me any time, just by telling the cops how we planned to keep in touch through the newspaper. Then all they'd have had to do was put the All Clear ad in the *Globe,* and I'd have run right into their arms. Rick may have robbed banks, but he's a lot straighter than any cops or bank presidents you're likely to find."

"What good will it do Rick for you to get yourself killed?" asked Harry.

"I'll get back at them!" Tony's eyes gleamed brighter.

"What about us?"

"You go on home. You're kids."

Harry planted himself right in front of Tony. Draped in a big old overcoat that hung to his ankles, and with a stocking cap pulled down over his ears, he looked like Dopey of the Seven Dwarfs, but he drew himself up to his tallest and looked Tony straight in the eye.

"We may be kids," he said in his husky voice, "but we've stood by you too. We've taken a lot of risks to keep you safe. It'll be awful for us if you just stay here and let yourself get killed, and not because the Evil Eye will be sure to find out how we've helped you and give us the treatment. We can take that. We have before. What we can't take, Tony," Harry's voice cracked and faltered, but he went on again, still looking Tony straight in the eye, "is for you to give up when you don't have to, because we can help you get away, and you are all we care about, and we thought you cared about us too."

Tony stared down at Harry, so dumpy and comical and yet, despite his funny clothes and twisted gnome's face, so bold and somehow noble. The gleam went out of Tony's eyes. He blinked and rubbed them, turned away, and began to pace up and down. "O.K., you win," he said with a nod at Harry and a half smile. "What's your plan?"

Harry cleared his throat. "First, we'll clean this place out so that, if they do find it, they'll never guess

182

you've just been here. Con and I will go home as usual. After dark, you'll go down to cousin Grace Tarlton's house where Phoebe lives, and you'll wait in the back yard behind the bushes until Phoebe comes out and takes you up to her Eagle's Nest; and you'll hide in it until Phoebe can get her mother's car, without her mother's knowing — it won't be hard, her mother's almost never home — and drive you to Paxton. You can get a bus there and go off somewhere and hide. You can write to the box number to let us know where you are, the way you did before, and we'll let you know when it's safe to come back, and we'll think of ways to keep them from sending us to Switzerland. You can count on us."

Tony shook his head. "That's some plan," he said, "but I'm not going anywhere near cousin Grace Tarlton. I remember her. She's the nosiest woman in town."

"She won't see you," replied Harry. "Phoebe, explain to Tony about your Eagle's Nest, the way you did to me."

Phoebe explained and, with Harry urging her on, admitted reluctantly that she could do all the things the plan demanded of her.

"I won't stay cooped up there for long," declared Tony.

"You won't have to," Harry reassured him. "You can probably leave on Monday."

"O.K.," Tony sighed, "if you say so."

They set right to work, for it was already midafternoon, and they were glad to be able to move about and get warm.

They carried all of Tony's gear, except what he was

183

taking with him, to the edge of the woods above Dream-wold Castle and left it there until Constance and Harry, with help from Ida, could take it into the house after dark. There, Ida would dispose of it. Back at the Secret Place, they emptied the ashes from the stove, and Constance and Phoebe poured water over it to make it rusty and sprinkled dirt over it and over the chairs and table and over Tony's bunk, so everything looked as if it had been standing unused for years. Tony and Harry ripped out some of the shelves so they would look as if they had fallen apart from rot and age. They swept the floor and sprinkled it with fresh dirt and water. They carefully swept and washed away all traces of footprints around the various entrances to the Secret Place and in the Nook. Finally they carried the ladder to the edge of the woods where the rest of the gear was stashed. It was getting late. Tony kissed Constance and Harry good-bye.

"Just one more thing," said Harry. "Will you give me the pistol to keep until you get back?"

"No," said Tony. "I may need it."

"Please. I'll give it back."

Tony shook his head. "I know you think I'll get scared and start shooting people up. I promise I won't use it for anything like that." He patted Harry's shoulder and gave him a gentle shove toward the house.

As they often had before, Tony and Phoebe watched the other two go in the back door, then they skirted the woods to the foot of the Tarlton Trail and parted. Tony would start for Miss Tarlton's house as soon as it got dark.

[30]

"WHERE HAVE YOU BEEN?" cried Miranda. "I was worried."

Phoebe opened her mouth to start on a new series of lies, but Miranda didn't give her time.

"You'll never guess who's been here!" she exclaimed, and went on, hardly giving herself time to breathe, "Charlotte and Ben! And you'll never guess why they came! To tell us they are getting married! Isn't that lovely?" And she burst into tears.

While Phoebe dispensed comfort and Kleenex, Miranda told her the events of the day. Charlotte had brought the bridesmaids' dresses for Phoebe and Miranda — rose taffeta and tulle, with ballerina skirts — all basted and ready to try on, and they'd tried to telephone Phoebe at Dreamwold Castle, but as usual they couldn't rouse anyone there, and Charlotte had been so disappointed because the wedding was to be in May, and Charlotte had her own dress to finish too.

Charlotte and Ben had decided to spend their honeymoon at the Mottrell Arms so they could be near Phoebe and Miranda, and Ben had taken them there to lunch, and made the reservations, and Miranda had been so happy for them both that she hadn't said a word about her own disappointment because she didn't want to spoil the day for them. Miranda managed a triumphant smile and then choked. "At the very end of the day, I couldn't hold myself in any longer, and I started to cry like a silly baby, and I told Charlotte all about Charles. Charlotte wanted to stay here with me, but Ben made her go back with him. She made him promise to bring her out again soon, but I'm not sure that he will. I know he was furious with me for upsetting Charlotte, but he couldn't be more furious than I am with myself!" Miranda dissolved in more tears.

It was a long time before Phoebe could persuade her to drink a cup of tea and eat a little supper. It had already been dark for several hours when Miranda agreed to take an aspirin and go to bed, and then she insisted on sitting up and looking over her thesis (to quiet her nerves, she said) for another hour before she finally turned off the light and went to sleep.

Phoebe got the key to the Eagle's Nest out of her drawer and tiptoed down the backstairs. In Miss Tarlton's part of the house, all was dark and quiet. Phoebe slipped out the back door. A shadow moved out of the shrubbery. It was Tony with a knapsack and a bag.

"I thought you'd never come," he whispered.

Phoebe led him into the house and up the backstairs to the apartment. As they were tiptoeing down the hall, Miranda moaned and then cried out. They froze and waited. Miranda made no more sounds, and they tiptoed on. Phoebe unlocked the door to the Eagle's Nest, gave Tony the key, and led him up the stairs. By the light from the hall below, they could see the circle of windows and the armchair.

"O.K.," whispered Tony, "but I've got to get out sometimes."

Phoebe whispered back that whenever the coast was clear, she'd tap three times, and then Tony could come down into the apartment. They thought they heard Miranda moan again.

"Scram," whispered Tony. "I'm all right."

Phoebe tiptoed down the stairs and closed the door. She heard Tony turn the key on the inside.

As she climbed into bed, she was sure she could never go to sleep, but the next thing she knew, it was morning, and very late. Miranda had had breakfast long ago. She had spread out her thesis on the parlor table and was sitting there with a fine view of the door to the Eagle's Nest. She sat there all morning. At noon, she went to the kitchen to eat lunch, and returned immediately to her work in the parlor. Phoebe suggested that she should take a nap, or, better still, a walk in the fresh air. Miranda replied that Phoebe was a dear to be so considerate, but she wasn't a bit sleepy, and it wasn't very good walking weather because it had begun to rain. Not until Miranda was in bed and asleep that night was Phoebe able to tap on the door to the Eagle's Nest. She had fixed a plate of food and some coffee for Tony. While he ate and drank they sat on the steps with the door ajar so they could hear any sounds Miranda might make.

"I've got to get out of here," whispered Tony.

Phoebe whispered back that Constance would tell her in school tomorrow if Harry thought it was safe for Tony to leave, and, if it was, she would drive him to Paxton in the afternoon.

"I'm leaving anyway," Tony whispered back, "no matter what Harry says. I feel like an animal in a cage, and it's cold, and the windows leak. Haven't you got a blanket or something?"

Phoebe hurried off to fetch the quilt off her bed. She remembered the electric heater in the bathroom. She was sure Miranda wouldn't notice that it was gone. She fetched it along with the quilt and plugged it in for Tony. She also explained to him that tomorrow wouldn't be so bad as today. After nine o'clock, when Miss Tarlton left for the Historical Society, the house would be empty. Tony could come down, get himself some breakfast, wash, shave, and stay in the apartment until noon. Then he'd better get back up into the Eagle's Nest because Miss Tarlton might come back for lunch. Phoebe herself would come home as soon as possible after school. Tony stretched out on the quilt in front of the heater, which was already giving out a warm glow.

"You're a good kid," he whispered. "Scram now. We both need some sleep. Tomorrow is the big day."

The next morning, Phoebe didn't get a chance to talk to Tony before she left for school. It was a cold, windy day, spitting rain. She was glad she had thought of the heater. Between classes, she and Constance exchanged nods and winks, but it wasn't until lunch that they could talk.

"How is he?" whispered Constance when they were settled at their corner table.

Phoebe whispered back her report.

"There's been merry hell up at Dreamwold Castle." Constance's eyes flashed. "We've made monkeys of them all — Evil Eye, Gestapo, cops, helicopter, bloodhounds." She grinned her buccaneer's grin and took a large bite of

188

tuna Newburg. "They started off early in the morning. First we heard the helicopter buzzing around. We even saw it a few times, flying very low. They found the Secret Place. At least one of them fell into it. He broke his leg. Had to be carried down on a stretcher." Constance tried to repress her giggles, but couldn't. She went on merrily, lapsing often into more giggles. "We'd done such a good job of cleaning up that they were sure nobody had been near the Secret Place for years. Then they fanned out and searched the whole mountain. The dogs must have picked up Old Foxy's scent or the vixen's because we could hear them yapping and baying all over the place, and the men yelling at them to come back." Phoebe began to giggle too.

"Finally," Constance went on, her eyes streaming with tears of mirth, "the whole bunch drove up to Dreamwold Castle in about ten cars with the sirens going full blast. We listened while they talked to the Evil Eye. That's how we know everything that happened. They wanted to search Dreamwold Castle too. The Evil Eye was livid, but they had a warrant, and he couldn't stop them. They ransacked the place, and they questioned Gestapo for two hours, until he was practically crying because he didn't know anything, and he's too dumb to make anything up. You should have heard them trying to question Ida!" The giggles overwhelmed Constance. After a long seizure, she gulped, wiped her eyes, and was able to go on. "Ida really told them off for messing up her kitchen. Even Harry and I couldn't understand everything she said, but she really scared those cops. They couldn't get out fast enough. I don't know what

she'd done with Tony's gear, but they never found it."
Constance took a deep breath. "They didn't get anything
out of Harry or me either. Harry did a lot of coughing
and wheezing and gasping as if he was too weak to talk.
I just acted sort of sweet and dumb." Constance took
another mouthful of tuna Newburg.

"They sent away the dogs and the helicopter yesterday afternoon, but they've left two men. watching the
Secret Place, in case Tony turns up, and I've got orders
for you. Harry says you are to drive Tony to Paxton this
afternoon. You are to take the Old Paxton Road because
there's hardly any traffic on it. You and Tony are to wear
hats and coats that you'll borrow from your mother, so
you'll look like two ladies out for a drive. Tony is to
write to the post box as soon as he can and give us an
address, so we can write to him and tell him when it's
safe to come back." Constance paused to think. "Oh
yes, I'll tell the proctor at afternoon study hall that you
have special permission to work in the library, so you
can leave right now and get the car back in plenty of
time, so your mother won't have missed it. O.K.?" Constance grinned.

"O.K.," Phoebe grinned back, although she trembled
inwardly at the thought of all she had to do that afternoon.

"I wish I was cool like you," said Constance. "I wish
I could drive the getaway car." The bell rang. They
gathered up their books. "So long." Constance waved
and left.

[31]

Phoebe slipped out of the school. The weather had gotten worse since morning. She ran for home through rain and a gusty wind that sent shivers through her. As she opened the back door, Miss Tarlton rushed forth to meet her.

"I am so glad you have come," she cried. "You know the terrible presentiments I've had about Charles and his trip! Charles laughed at me, but now I know I was right! Bess is walking!" Miss Tarlton stared at Phoebe with eyes no longer steely, but watery, distraught, pleading. "Bess is trying to warn me about Charles. Please don't laugh at me. Help me!"

"Bess? You mean the ghost?"

"Who else?" cried Miss Tarlton. "I came home early from the Society this morning because I had the presentiment worse than ever, and no one comes to the Historical Rooms in such bad weather anyway." She reached out and seized Phoebe's hand. "No sooner had I come in the front door than I heard Bess's footsteps going back and forth on the third floor, then I heard her sloshing out the water from her bucket. I telephoned Charles's airline at once, but I couldn't make anyone listen to me. Then I telephoned my cousin, the Judge, and he laughed at me."

"Did you go up to the third floor to make sure that no one was there?"

"Yes. After I'd telephoned, I went up. I hoped maybe Bess would tell me more and help me."

"Are you sure that no one, I mean no real person, was there?"

"Of course I am." She gave Phoebe's hand an impatient jerk. "How can I reach Charles in time to warn him? I am too worried to think straight. Please help me."

Phoebe could have collapsed in relief right there at Miss Tarlton's feet, but she knew she must think of someone, someone outside, away from the house, to whom she could send Miss Tarlton for help. She racked her brain.

"How about Mr. Bartlett?"

"What a good idea! I knew you would help me! I'll telephone him now."

Miss Tarlton gave Phoebe's hand a squeeze and dropped it and set off for the kitchen.

"I think it would be better if you went to see him," cried Phoebe.

Miss Tarlton stopped short. "You are right. If I'm standing in front of him, he won't dare to laugh at me. I'll make him telephone the airline, and they'll listen to him!"

She disappeared and returned at once with her coat half on and her hat askew. Phoebe helped her with the coat. "You are a good child," said Miss Tarlton, breathing hard and struggling with the coat. "Don't be afraid to go up to Bess. She loves children. I wish you were a Tarlton. Then you might hear her." She dashed out the door and left it banging. As she crossed the yard, her hat blew off, but she didn't stop to pick it up. She scurried off into the wind, hair flying, coat flapping, like some old bird trying to take off. Phoebe shut the door. She felt too weak and exhausted to go out and recover the hat. It was all she could do to get upstairs.

She tapped three times at the door to the Eagle's Nest. Tony opened at once. He was holding the quilt around him because he had no clothes on.

"Are the cops coming?"

"No, you're safe. She thought you were her family ghost," and Phoebe collapsed on the bottom step. She began to giggle and couldn't stop.

Tony glared at her as if he thought she was giggling at him. Then slowly he smiled. "You mean she thought I was the old black lady with the buckets of water?"

Phoebe nodded and between giggles managed to explain how she had sent Miss Tarlton away. Tony smiled again.

"The Tarltons are awfully proud of that ghost of theirs. I remember cousin Grace boasting about her when I was a kid. She wanted to make us jealous because we didn't have a ghost up at Dreamwold Castle." Tony drew a deep breath and let it out with a whistle. "That was a close shave. I'd been hanging around all morning, and I thought I still had a lot of time to kill, so I started to take a bath. Then I heard cousin Grace calling 'Yoo hoo!' I knew her voice right off. I remember it from the old days when she used to come to see my mother and talk so much. Next I heard her coming up the stairs. I stuffed my clothes in the hamper and ran for it. I wonder what cousin Grace would have thought, if she'd bumped

193

into me running raw down the hall?" He began to laugh as he hadn't for days, and Phoebe laughed too.

Tony turned serious. "I've got to get out of here. What does Harry say?" Phoebe told him, and in a few minutes he was dressed and packed and ready to go. They locked the door to the Eagle's Nest, and Phoebe put the key back in her bureau drawer. The keys to the Goldfinch were in the dish on the hall table as usual. None of Miranda's coats would fit over Tony's shoulders, so they settled for one of her hats. Phoebe put on another. They couldn't help grinning at each other, they looked so funny.

Once in the Goldfinch and on their way, nothing seemed funny anymore. Tony sat hunched down in his seat and stared straight ahead. His face was grim. Phoebe could hardly remember how to drive. She stalled the engine, ground the gears, and even went backward when she meant to go forward. Each blunder made her shakier. However, by taking side streets they got onto the Old Paxton Road without having to pass Mr. Wade, and this time no one bumped into them. When they were clear of the town, Tony straightened up, but he didn't say anything, and Phoebe was just as glad. Although there was almost no traffic on the Old Paxton Road, there were enough hills and twists and bends and potholes, not to mention the rain, to keep Phoebe occupied and not a little scared all the way to the outskirts of Paxton — which, on this road, was a two-hour drive. As she drove on and on, her head and back began to ache, and her throat got scratchy and dry. At the first traffic light, Tony finally spoke.

"I'll get out here and walk to the bus station. If you go farther into town, you may get in trouble in the traffic. If you start right home from here, you'll surely make it before five, and you'd better check your Eagle's Nest. I think I left the heater plugged in."

Phoebe was glad to pull in to the side of the road. Tony took off Miranda's hat and laid it on the seat beside him.

"Thanks for everything," he said. "You did a good job."

"I'm sorry I can't drive better."

"You drive O.K." Tony smiled at her briefly, then stared off in front of him. "I ought to scram," he said, but he still sat.

"Where will you go?"

Tony shrugged, "It doesn't matter."

"You'll write to us at the post box, won't you, as soon as you know where you're staying?"

Tony nodded.

"As soon as it's safe, we'll tell you, and you can come back, and then — "

"Let's not talk about that," said Tony. "I've got to scram along."

"But you will come back, Tony, won't you?"

"I'll try." Tony gave her another brief smile. "Say good-bye to Harry and Con for me, and Ida too. Tell them to remember me the way I am in the woods, not the other way." Still he made no move to leave.

"We'll all be remembering you and waiting for you."

"Don't count too much on . . . on anything." He drew a deep breath and opened the car door, then he leaned toward Phoebe, put his arm around her shoulder, and kissed her cheek. "You're a good kid, one of the best. I wish I was like you." He climbed quickly out of the car, shouldered his knapsack, picked up his bag, waved, and walked away into the rain.

[32]

WHILE PHOEBE WAS DRIVING back to Denby, the rain let up, the wind blew rents in the clouds, and the sun flashed out. She should have found the trip easier, but it seemed harder and longer. Her head and back ached worse. Her throat hurt. It was an effort to keep her eyes on the road and to steer. When she finally had eased the Goldfinch into Miss Tarlton's shed, she leaned back and shut her eyes and felt she could have sat there forever. The very thought of climbing up to the apartment exhausted her. However, she made herself get out of the car, took the two hats and the keys, which seemed extraordinarily heavy, and crossed the yard to the back door. As she opened it, a cloud of smoke billowed out and almost smothered her. She stood appalled, unable to move or think, while more smoke poured out and the wind snatched it up and whipped and whirled it past her into the yard. From inside the house came a bang as if a cannon had gone off. Then came a roaring. A tongue of flame darted down the backstairs and almost caught Phoebe's skirt. She dropped the hats and the keys and ran screaming across the yard and down the street straight into Miranda, who was coming home from school. Phoebe could never remember clearly what happened after that. The fire engines clanged and wailed until her ears rang and her head ached worse than ever. The firemen shoved back Phoebe and Miranda and the crowd that had gathered, while they squirted Miss Tarlton's house with their hoses. Oceans of smoke billowed out. Phoebe could hardly breathe. Her eyes stung, her throat burned. Once, through the smoke, she saw Miss Tarlton trying to rush into her house and being held back by firemen. Miss Tarlton screamed a terrible scream which pierced Phoebe's heart.

Like a genie, Miss Dwight appeared out of a puff of smoke. She led Phoebe and Miranda off to the school and into a room full of small white beds. It was the infirmary, and they could stay there for the night. As soon as Miss Dwight left them, Phoebe lay down on one of the beds. She told Miranda she didn't want any supper. She'd just stay where she was. She shut her eyes, but no sleep came. Instead came waves of hustling, bustling, whispering people. They stuck a thermometer into Phoebe's mouth, they wrestled her out of her clothes and into a sort of nightgown. They poked pills down her burning throat and then offered her soothing drinks that didn't soothe. She turned away to sleep, and then the running began. She ran, leaden-footed, round and round, never reaching her goal, never shaking off the horror at her heels. When she screamed in mortal fear that the thing was about to overtake her and grab her, no sound came, and she woke up to her burning throat and pounding head, and to find Miranda or the school nurse be-

197

side her, offering more pills and drinks, and she turned away and shut her eyes, and the running began again. It seemed to go on for days.

When, at length, the pounding in her head let up, and the soothing drinks began to soothe the burning in her throat, Phoebe felt no desire to move. She was content to lie in her bed and fall in and out of a mercifully dreamless doze. Once, as she was waking up, the nurse told her that she had got well just in time. The school was closing for spring vacation, and the nurse herself was about to leave, but Miss Dwight was letting Phoebe and Miranda stay on in the infirmary until their new quarters were ready. Since Phoebe was so much better, Miranda could look after her, and she wouldn't have to be sent to the hospital. She could thank her lucky stars and the new miracle drugs for that. In the olden days she'd have been flat on her back for months, maybe forever. The nurse said good-bye, and Phoebe fell back to sleep. A few days later, the doctor paid a visit and pronounced her cured. Miranda bought a steak and a pecan pie for supper, to celebrate, and after they had eaten them in the infirmary kitchen, Miranda suggested a short stroll around the school grounds, so Phoebe could get the feel of her legs again.

The evening was warm. Almost all the trees had come into full summer leaf, and among them Phoebe thought she heard a thrush singing. High in the darkening sky, two hawks sailed by, heading toward Old Mott. Phoebe wondered if they were Mr. and Mrs. Red Tail hurrying home to see how the young ones were getting on. For the first time since she had taken sick, the excitement of the days with Tony on the mountain stirred again inside her. It must have been a week since Tony left. Surely there was a letter in the box. She would collect it tomorrow, first thing, and take it up to Dreamwold Castle. She and Constance and Harry would read it together. It occurred to her that they didn't even know how the getaway had come off. Constance had probably tried to see her in the infirmary and been turned away. How anxiously she and Harry must be waiting for her!

"Now that you are well," said Miranda, "I must have a serious talk with you."

"What about?" Grudgingly, Phoebe yanked her thoughts back from Dreamwold Castle.

"Your school work." Miranda cleared her throat. "Miss Dwight tells me that you haven't been doing your homework and are failing in all your subjects."

Phoebe groaned. Miranda laid a hand on her shoulder.

"I know that I'm largely to blame because I've neglected you, and Miss Dwight realizes that she made a mistake in letting you take those afternoon walks. She should have started you right in on extra supervised study, but," Miranda's voice turned businesslike and she rapped gently on Phoebe's shoulder for emphasis, "only you can make up the work. We can't do it for you. To make your job easier, Miss Dwight has arranged for you to be excused from gym so you can have tutoring and supervised study every afternoon."

"But Miranda!"

"Miss Dwight says this is necessary. She wouldn't go to so much trouble about you, if she weren't convinced that you are capable of doing good work. In the evenings," Miranda's voice softened, "you and I will do our homework together, the way we used to. I won't be going out anymore. Every spare minute I'll be working on my thesis. Miss Dwight is being very generous. She is giving us an attic room in the boarding department. They usually keep the trunks in it, but they are painting it up for us, and it will be quite nice. I'll do some proctoring to pay for the room, and we'll take our meals with the boarders. All this should make it easier for us both to study."

After a pause, Miranda said, "Do you realize that the only thing we saved from the fire was my thesis, and that was only because I had taken it to Miss Dwight to get her opinion on it. She thinks it is very good, and we both think it was providential that the thesis wasn't burned with everything else. I am going to make a special effort to finish it and get my degree this summer. If I do, Miss Dwight promises to give me a permament job and make me head of the History Department. I'm going to show her what I can do!" Miranda gave her head a determined toss. Phoebe didn't say anything.

"There's another thing I didn't want to tell you until you were better. The poor old Goldfinch was too badly burned to repair. No one thought to take it out of the shed, and that went up like a matchbox. We'll get the insurance money sometime, of course, but, oh dear, I had so counted on driving to Putnam Park for part of this vacation to help Charlotte get ready. I do so want her to have a beautiful wedding, and I want to make up to her for the day they came here and I spoiled all her happiness by telling her about that miserable affair of mine." Miranda walked on with bent head. She turned to Phoebe again. "I haven't even told her about the fire or your being sick. I didn't want to be a burden to her, and you know how hard it is to tell her anything over the phone. She always cries." Miranda got out her handkerchief and blew her nose.

"Maybe she and Ben will drive out again soon, and you can tell her everything," said Phoebe.

"I don't know." Miranda sounded sadder than ever. "Ben was so cross with me that day. Maybe he'll never drive her out again."

Phoebe bowed her head.

"You must get right to bed," announced Miranda, firm and businesslike again, "and I must get to work. After I've finished the thesis and you've finished summer school, maybe we can take a vacation. We'll surely have a new car by then." She gave Phoebe an encouraging little pat.

"Summer school!"

"I guess I forgot to tell you. Miss Dwight says that you should certainly go to summer school, and it's only for six weeks."

"Who does Miss Dwight think she is?" shouted Phoebe. "God?"

"Of course not, Phoebe, and don't shout!" After a minute Miranda added, "For us, now, come to think of it, she just about *is* God, and I think we'd better do what she tells us to."

[33]

NEXT MORNING, just as she had expected, Phoebe found a letter in the post box. With it tucked in her pocket, she made her usual detour through town and set off up the road to Dreamwold Castle. Today, the driveway, which she had last seen bordered by banks of snow, wound through cascades of blossoming shrubs, and the house, swathed and garlanded in spring blossoms, looked like neither the library at Miranda's college nor the Thyangboche Lamasery, but like a real dreamcastle, floating on clouds of pink and white and lavender. Phoebe hurried around to the kitchen door and knocked. Then, remembering that Ida was deaf, she pushed the door open and went inside. The kitchen looked bigger and emptier than she remembered. Ida's cozy corner was gone, and for a minute she couldn't see Ida anywhere. Then she spotted her in a far corner, taking dishes out of a cupboard and packing them into a barrel.

"Ida!" she shouted.

Ida turned, shouted something, and made for Phoebe with her arms widespread. Her uniform and apron crackled as crisply as ever, and her rosy old face twitched, but when she came up to Phoebe, she threw herself on her neck and burst into tears. Ida sobbed on and on, and at intervals made long, earnest speeches to which Phoebe could only respond with nods and pats and sympathetic noises. At length Ida grew calmer, went to the dumbwaiter, shouted up it, and proceeded to haul Phoebe up. Phoebe climbed out into Harry's attic. Constance and Harry stood together facing her. Neither one looked very glad to see her.

"It's about time," said Constance.

"I've been sick. I thought you knew."

"I guess I did, but I forgot." Constance sounded as if she didn't much care.

"I brought a letter from Tony." Phoebe held it out and hoped that one of them at least would smile, or maybe even say, "Thank you."

They turned and looked at each other. After a minute, Harry stepped forward and took the letter. He opened it and read it slowly, then he handed it to Constance, turned his back, and walked away. It took Constance even longer to read the letter. When she finally finished, she dropped her hands to her sides and bent her head. Tears streamed down her face.

"What's the matter?" demanded Phoebe. "Can't I see the letter too? I'm a member of the Band."

No one answered her. At last Harry turned back to Constance.

"Give her the letter," he said. "He meant it for her too."

Constance handed over the letter, and Phoebe read:

DEAR KIDS:

I'VE GOT THIS FAR, AND I'VE TRIED LIKE HARRY SAID, BUT I CAN'T TAKE IT. I CAN'T TAKE BEING COOPED UP IN ROOMS IN CITIES ANY MORE THAN OLD FOXY COULD. I CAN'T TAKE HIDING OUT AND RUNNING SCARED. I CAN'T TAKE IT IN THE JUG EITHER. I'VE BEEN THERE, SO I KNOW. YOU ARE ALL SWELL KIDS, THE VERY BEST, AND WE HAD A SWELL TIME ON THE MOUNTAIN. IT WAS THE BEST TIME I EVER

HAD. BUT IT'S OVER. IF I WAS TO COME BACK NOW, I'D JUST GET YOU IN TROUBLE, AND NO MATTER WHAT HARRY THINKS, YOU ARE BETTER OFF WITHOUT ME. I WANT YOU KIDS TO GROW UP DIFFERENT FROM ME BECAUSE THE WAY I AM DOESN'T WORK. MAYBE IF YOU STICK WITH THE EVIL EYE AND SCHOOL A LITTLE LONGER THAN I DID, YOU'LL FIGURE OUT SOME WAY TO GET ALONG WITH THEM AND BE FREE AND INDEPENDENT TOO. I WANT YOU TO GIVE IT A TRY, AND WHEN IT GETS TOUGH, GO UP ON THE MOUNTAIN AND REMEMBER ME AND COME BACK AND TRY HARDER.

I DON'T WANT TO DISGRACE THE FAMILY ANY MORE THAN I HAVE ALREADY. IF THEY WANT TO CALL THIS AN ACCIDENT, THEY CAN, BUT I WANT YOU TO KNOW THE TRUTH. IF THERE WAS ANY OTHER WAY OUT FOR ME, I'D TAKE IT. BELIEVE ME AND DO LIKE I'VE TOLD YOU.

LOVE,

TONY

"I don't understand." Phoebe looked from Harry to Constance and back.

"He shot himself," said Harry. "He shot himself four days ago." His voice broke. He turned abruptly and started walking again.

Phoebe stood staring at the letter, and the tears that welled up in her eyes blurred Tony's writing.

Harry stopped in front of Constance. "I knew I should get the gun away from him. I told you when it happened it wasn't an accident."

Constance nodded and swallowed a sob.

"He was sad when I left him in Paxton," said Phoebe, "but I never thought — "

"Of course you didn't," returned Harry. "Even I didn't, but I should have got the gun away from him anyway."

The dumbwaiter began to rattle. Harry stuck his head into the shaft and exchanged shouts with Ida.

"She says they're coming for the trunk in an hour, and we'd better have it packed or the Evil Eye will get another heart attack."

"I wish he would!" exclaimed Constance, then she slapped her hand over her mouth. "No, I don't. I'll try to put up with him because Tony says to."

"Then you'd better decide fast what you're taking," returned Harry. "My stuff's all in."

For the first time, Phoebe noticed an open trunk where Nanga Parbat had been. There was a litter of clothes and books on the floor around it. In a corner, under sheets, she recognized the shapes of Everest and Nanga Parbat.

"Are you going away?"

Harry nodded.

"Where?"

"Switzerland."

"I thought you could always get out of that."

Harry shrugged. "Why bother? We might as well be there as here, now that Tony's dead. We'll have a good chance to learn to put up with the Evil Eye, I mean the Old Man, and Barbara. They're coming, too, so the Old Man can get over his heart attack. He's not going to run for governor. He's going to try to be friends with us, to make up for Tony."

"You've taken up all the room. I can't fit my stuff in," shouted Constance. She was on her knees beside the trunk. She scowled at Harry.

"Maybe Ida can fit some of your stuff in with hers," suggested Harry.

"Is Ida going too?" asked Phoebe.

Harry nodded. "The Evil Eye, I mean the Old Man, is giving her a trip to Finland to visit her relatives, and he hopes she'll stay there. She doesn't want to. She wants to go to boarding school with us." Harry gave a sour smile. "Did she cry all over you?"

Phoebe nodded.

"She's in an awful state, but I don't see how we can take her to boarding school. She'll have to make out somehow."

"What about me?" asked Phoebe.

"What about you?" repeated Harry, as if he didn't understand.

"What will I do when you're gone?"

"Whatever you did before, I guess."

"Oh Harry, I've got to live inside the school because our apartment burned down, and they're making me do extra school work every afternoon, and then go to summer school, and Tony is never coming back, and all I have is Con and you. If you go away — " Phoebe couldn't keep her voice steady any longer.

Ida burst into the room. She was flushed and tearful. She and Constance and Harry shouted at each other while they snatched things out of the trunk and stuffed other things in.

Constance shoved Harry aside. "Get the stuff out of my bedroom," she said. "You're just in the way here."

"O.K.," replied Harry, "but keep your shirt on, can't you?" He started for the door and noticed Phoebe again. "Look," he said, "the men are here for the trunk already. You better give me the letter and get going." Phoebe handed him the letter. "Thanks for bringing it," he said.

"Maybe we'll see you again some time, when we come back, if we ever do. Good-bye, and good luck and thanks for helping us." Harry nodded and left.

Phoebe watched Constance and Ida for a minute. "Good-bye," she said. When Constance didn't answer, she said again, louder, "I guess I've got to go. Good-bye."

"Oh, good-bye," Constance flapped her hand in Phoebe's general direction and went on stuffing things into the trunk or handing them to Ida, who talked vociferously and unintelligibly all the time.

Since it was clear to her that no one was going to let her down in the dumbwaiter, Phoebe took the backstairs. After a few false turns, she found her way to the kitchen. She left, as she had come, by the back door.

When she got to the business block in town, Phoebe remembered to take her detour to avoid Mr. Wade, but she forgot that she lived at the school now, and she suddenly found herself in front of what had been Miss Tarlton's house. The walls still stood, blackened, blistered, and in places charred right through. Behind the black-rimmed, shattered front windows, hung a few shreds of curtain, and behind them Phoebe could make out piles of rubbish in what had been Miss Tarlton's front parlor. A smell of smoke, wet dust, and ashes tainted the air. Phoebe turned away toward the school, only to meet Miss Tarlton. She looked very old and sad, but her face lighted up as soon as she spotted Phoebe.

"You see, I was right." She seized Phoebe by the arm. "Bess *was* warning me, but I misunderstood her. I thought she was warning me about Charles, but it was really about the bad wiring in the house." For a minute

207

she looked up at the ruined façade, then turned quickly back to Phoebe. "It was so beautiful," she said, "and it was always my home. Nobody else in Denby had a house like mine, or a ghost like Bess. Now we are both homeless — two poor old homeless ghosts."

"You're not a ghost, Miss Tarlton."

"You are kind to say so, my dear, but I feel like one. I have no place in the world anymore." Miss Tarlton sighed, then managed a faint smile. "Charles is very kind to me, as always. He has telegraphed to ask me to visit him in Japan, and all my other relatives are urging me to go. Do you think I should?"

"Yes," replied Phoebe. "The trip will help you to forget about your house."

"I think that is just what my relatives here want," returned Miss Tarlton, and a spark of the old icy fire gleamed in her eye. "They don't want me nagging at them to raise the funds to rebuild. It could be done, you know. There is a copy of the original plan in my box at the bank."

Phoebe racked her brain for a comforting reply to that. "Perhaps, if you go away for a while, your relatives will get to feel different," was the best she could do, but it satisfied Miss Tarlton.

"You always were a sensible girl," replied Miss Tarlton, "and you may be right." She leaned closer to Phoebe. "There is something I haven't told anyone, but I want to tell you. That oldest Mottrell boy, the bad one, shot himself by accident in a hotel room somewhere, just three days after Bess gave her warning. I believe she was warning about him, too."

Suddenly Phoebe saw Tony standing at the foot of the steps to the Eagle's Nest, wrapped in her bed quilt and laughing. She wondered if that was the last time he had laughed, and she herself could hardly keep from crying.

Controlling herself, she said, "But Bess was a Tarlton ghost. She wouldn't warn for a Mottrell."

"You forget one thing, my dear." Miss Tarlton leaned closer still. "That Mottrell boy's first name was Tarlton. You couldn't fool Bess!" She gave Phoebe a tremendous wink then stepped back and eyed her slantwise. "You don't think I'm crazy, do you?"

"Oh, no."

"I think some of my relatives do," returned Miss Tarlton. She glanced around her. "I must go, or one of them will come after me. It annoys them to see me standing around here." She shook Phoebe's hand. "It's been a pleasure to know you. I'll send you postcards from Japan."

[34]

PHOEBE TRUDGED ON toward the school, where, under the eye of Miss Dwight, she was doomed, it seemed — in loneliness and at hard labor — to serve out her days. She did not see the red-white-and-blue taxi in front of the school gate until, having crossed the street, she almost walked into it. Ben was smiling at her out of the driver's window. He looked solid and kind and friendly; and she wished she hadn't had to pretend not to know him up there on the mountain. She dropped her eyes in embarrassment.

"It's good to see you, Skibootch," said Ben, "especially because last time I was here a funny thing happened up by that old tin mine we went to in the autumn, and I want to tell you about it."

Phoebe wondered how she was going to lie her way out of this, and suddenly it came to her, in a wave of relief, that she didn't need to lie anymore. She could tell Ben everything. He would understand, if anyone would, and if he blamed her for all she had done and was angry, it would still be better to have the whole business out in the open and to take what was coming to her. She drew a deep breath and looked Ben straight in the eye.

"I know what happened. It was me you saw, Tony and me."

"So, I was right! I knew I couldn't make a mistake like that, in spite of what Wade said!" He stared at Phoebe, his forehead all furrowed. "What did you run away from me for? Who is Tony?"

"I'll explain about him and everything," and although Phoebe wanted nothing so much as to start right in, she couldn't because suddenly she was starting to cry. "Everything went wrong," she mumbled. "I didn't care what awful things I did, like pretending not to know you, Ben, as long as it was for Tony and the Band, but it's ended up all wrong, and Harry and Constance are going away, and they don't care about me. I guess they never did. They don't even care much about Ida, just about each other and Tony, and, oh Ben, Tony's dead!"

Phoebe found herself sobbing, so that she couldn't go on.

Ben handed her a handkerchief and waited for her to control the sobs. He reached over and opened the door on the other side of the taxi and patted the seat beside him. "Hop in. I guess you've got a lot to get off your chest. Just take it easy and slow so I'll understand what you're talking about."

Phoebe climbed in beside him. It was comforting to be with him in his taxi the way she had been so often in the old days. "There's a lot to tell. It will take a long time."

"We've got plenty of that," replied Ben. "The girls are in there gabbing and trying on wedding clothes. They'll be at it till the cows come home, so spit it all out." Ben nodded and smiled.

Phoebe did — the whole story from the day she zapped the Fossil to her latest visit to Dreamwold Castle. Having told all, she felt better until she realized that Ben wasn't smiling anymore. Indeed she had never seen him look more serious. He didn't say anything to her at all.

"Do you think I was very bad?" she ventured.

Ben considered her sternly before he answered. "You were very foolish, daydreaming about Nepal instead of doing your homework, when you know perfectly well that a bunch of kids can't just hop off for a place like that. I thought you had more sense."

Phoebe felt her cheeks flush. "It all seemed possible when Harry was talking about it in his attic." Ben shook his head and looked sterner than ever. "And it was so miserable alone in the apartment."

"I guess it was," replied Ben, "but just the same, you've got to live in the real world, even when it's not much fun. You don't change things by fooling yourself." He turned sharply. "And you did some bad things — of course, those two put you up to them — but a smart girl like you that's been brought up among decent folks should know better than to snitch her mother's car and copy her mother's signature to deceive her and the post office, not to mention all the lying you did! And, at the end, I believe you harbored a criminal and helped him escape from justice." Ben drew a deep breath and opened his eyes wide, as if he were astonished at the depth and scope of Phoebe's badness.

"I was bad all right," she admitted, "but Tony," she laid her hand on Ben's arm and tried to look into his eyes and make him understand, "Tony wasn't a criminal. He just wanted to live free. If you'd known him — "

Ben patted her hand. "I understand how you feel about him, but he killed a man, and the law is the law."

"You mean I should go and tell everything to Mr. Wade?"

Ben spent a long time scowling, pursing and un-pursing his lips, and rubbing his chin before he answered. "No. Not now anyway. Tony's dead, and those twins and their father are trying to patch things up and behave better. I don't think Wade would want to stir up more trouble there."

Phoebe thought hard for a minute. "Then I'd like to tell everything to Miranda. I lied to her so, and I hated it, but once I'd started I couldn't stop. I'd feel better if she knew the truth."

"Yes," replied Ben, "you must tell Miranda. Only," and he paused again and wrinkled his forehead and rubbed his chin some more, "wait until after Charlotte and I are married. That wedding means a lot to Charlotte, and Miranda has troubled her enough already with her shenanigans without you — "

Phoebe bowed her head. "I'd never do anything to spoil the wedding for Charlotte."

"Of course you wouldn't." Ben sounded friendlier. After more thought he went on. "As soon as you and Miranda went off on your own, Charlotte started calling you the Babes in the Wood. It provoked me sometimes because she worried herself so about you two, but she was right. She knew you two couldn't make it alone. She has more sense than any of us."

Ben turned to Phoebe. "What would you say, if I told you that after we're married Charlotte and I are coming to live in Denby so we can keep an eye on you and Miranda?"

At first Phoebe couldn't say anything. She threw her arms around Ben and hugged him. "It's the best idea you ever had. It's what Miranda and I have always wanted."

Ben extricated himself from the hug. "Then that's what we're going to do. Only don't give me the credit. It's Charlotte's idea. She's been chipping away at me with it ever since we got engaged. I wouldn't hear of it. I said we'd live our life, and you two could look after yourselves, but now after what you've told me, I see how right she was. It works out for my business too, and for hers," Ben went on. "I need to expand, to invest my capital; and Denby needs a taxi service, just like Wade said. I'll have two businesses, one here and one there. And if the ladies in Denby are half as stylish and elegant as they're supposed to be, they'll snap up Charlotte's creations faster than she can sew them. She's a wonderful dressmaker." Ben looked as if he might burst with pride. He nudged Phoebe. "Run and tell her I've changed my mind about the Babes in the Wood. She'll be tickled pink."

Phoebe started to climb out, but Ben held her back. "Maybe on weekends, after you've done all that summer-school work, we can go into the woods together and you'll teach me some of the things Tony taught you. It will give you a change after all the studying you're going to have to do, and I'll learn a lot, and we'll think about Tony and remember him the way he wanted to be."

Again Phoebe was close to sobbing.

"Go on now," said Ben. "Run find Charlotte."